AGOAK
The Legacy of Agaguk

Yves Thériault
Translated by John David Allan

McGraw-Hill Ryerson Limited

Toronto   Montréal   New York   St. Louis   San Francisco
Auckland   Beirut   Bogotá   Düsseldorf   Johannesburg   Lisbon
London   Lucerne   Madrid   Mexico   New Delhi   Panama
Paris   San Juan   São Paulo   Singapore   Sydney   Tokyo

AGOAK
The Legacy of Agaguk

Canadian Cataloguing in Publication Data

Thériault, Yves, date
  [Agoak. English]
  Agoak

Translation of Agoak.
Sequel to Agaguk.

ISBN 0-07-082947-0 bd
ISBN 0-07-082934-9 pa

I. Title. II. Title: Agoak. English.

PS8539.H43A6513   C843'.5'4   C78-001636-X
PQ3919.T4A6513

1 2 3 4 5 6 7 8 9 10 D 8 7 6 5 4 3 2 1 0 9

Printed and bound in Canada

CONTENTS

PART ONE
THE ESKIMOS

CHAPTER I

When he had come of age, tested his mettle and set his sights on certain goals, Agoak donned the three-piece suit which people in Povungnituk said he wore so well, withdrew a good portion of his savings from the Caisse Populaire and left for Frobisher Bay, his future home. A bush plane belonging to a pilot friend took him as far as Fort Chimo. From there he travelled on the Nordair 737 which serves Frobisher Bay. Agoak arrived at his destination and had the Nanook taxi take him to the big building in the centre of town, a building taller than he might have imagined. He had been told at the airport it was the nerve centre of Frobisher, incorporating the hotel and related facilities, the shops, the bank and other key public meeting points of this Arctic settlement, whose very size suddenly alarmed Agoak a little. As his taxi travelled along the gravel road, he noticed numerous fuel-storage tanks of an imposing size, a baffling quantity of different antennas and a reddish-brown building marked Telesat. Here at last was one landmark he knew about — the place where all those aerial pulsations from the Anik satellite ended up. He also spotted the school and the offices of both the federal and territorial governments. A little dazed with having taken in so many sights so quickly, Agoak finally entered the hotel. He hadn't reserved a room, but it was the off-season. Summer was over and the approaching winter had begun to leave morning frosts and a chill in the air, portents of the misery to come, even if it was still more imagined than real.

Agoak was promptly given a room on the third floor of the six-floor hotel. He was dressed like a White and carefully groomed, and his English left nothing to be desired. Where doors were opened to Agoak, an Eskimo travelling by dog-team and reeking of seal and

1

rancid fish might well have been turned away. Agoak's stay in Moosonee, and his two study trips to Montreal and Toronto respectively, had taught him much about relations between Whites and Eskimos, as well as about the differences between the norms of the South and those of the North. He had a fairly stoical approach to his dealings with the Whites, such as they were, having learned to appreciate that everyone's personal development must move through trying and often unpredictable stages. As an Eskimo, he was in fact rather surprised at having been welcomed so warmly, a turn of events he attributed to his manner of dressing and the attention he paid to being neat, well-groomed and articulate in English. He was not unaware, however, of the way a full-blooded Inuk, a repository of the ancient traditions, could be treated on occasion. He had seen this for himself, even in Povungnituk, where Eskimo life was much less altered than it was here, or at Fort Chimo, or again, as he had been told, at Inuvik, far away to the west across the Top of the World.

In the spirit of his grandfather Agaguk (this grandfather who now seemed so remote!), Agoak was anxious to explore the new territory for himself. After freshening up in his room, shaving and preening as much as he thought necessary, he headed off on foot into the fresh, windy weather. He had begun by strolling around inside the hotel and shopping complex. Once outside he surveyed Frobisher itself down to the ground, doing perfect justice to his heritage. He looked over the town's amenities, put his nose to the wind and came very close to examining the ground for tracks, all in order to acquire a gut awareness of what this new world held in store for him, the pleasant surprises as well as the dangers.

The next day, satisfied that he had found a wavelength he could tune in to, Agoak began looking for work. He had devoted a whole day to locating the points of interest, the residential areas, the stores, business firms and the offices of the various governments. He knew where to find the hospital, the bars, the restaurants, the cafés, the local branch of the Bay and various other facilities. He had toured the different neighborhoods of the town and sized up some of their basic differences.

He was aware he didn't know everything about Frobisher, but he had learned enough to form a clear overall picture. He could live well in this place, and even prosper in it. Since returning to Povungnituk from his study trips, he had worked as a bookkeeper for the Eskimo Art Co-operative, and on several occasions had filled in for staff at the Caisse Populaire when they were on leave or holidays, or had taken ill. With this experience behind him, he turned up for an appointment at the Frobisher bank. He had not always been well-received elsewhere, but this time he hit it off with the manager. They got right down to business and two days later he began work as a teller, to become the virtually heaven-sent replacement for an employee who had grown weary of the Arctic and fled to the South without even collecting his final pay cheque.

Although he had just settled in, Agoak could already boast that he had cleared the first hurdle. Had old Agaguk not always secured his survival by first checking the lay of the land? Then, and only then, did he select a site for his dwelling. Agoak would follow his example.

Now, however, it was no longer a simple question, as it was in the old days for Agaguk, of wandering across the tundra until a location was found which accorded with the usual demands of the weather and the basic needs of life. For an Inuk immigrating to a town, other standards, those of the Whites, of civilization, of progress, created demands of another sort. Having been hired at the bank made Agoak eligible for a dwelling. However, the search for a roof had to be made through a particular agency. After making inquiries, Agoak learned he would have to meet the local officer in charge of accommodation. He was a man with problems and was constantly being bombarded by requests for shelter. He had at his disposal only a small housing quota, which could not be increased without the grudging approval of the Government of the Territories and its apathetic bureaucrats. They had the last say on the town council's expansion projects and more often than not withheld approval. Over a two day period, therefore, Agoak was forced to shunt back and forth from one bureaucrat to another, and start his laborious explanations from scratch each time. As might have been expected, he was immediately offered accommodations — in the form of a simple two-room apartment — in one of the buildings designed for new residents such as him. But Agoak knew he could claim for a house and it was to a house that he intended to bring Judith. Unfortunately, he was not yet married to the girl, so that administratively speaking, she did not exist. Otherwise she would have to be considered his common-law wife, and in the strict and puritanical outlook of the bureaucrats, this was unthinkable. In extreme cases, involving low-class Inuit laborers, such liaisons might be tolerated, but a bank teller was on a level with the White Man and, this being the case, it was essential that everything be in order, or as the expression had it — *legal and proper.*

"She must be your wife," the bureaucrat declared.

"She will be," said Agoak. "When I come back with her to take possession of my house."

"Of the house that will be allocated to you," the bureaucrat said, correcting him.

"Fine, as you wish. But when she gets here, we'll have been married in Povungnituk."

Finally, with less than good grace, they told Agoak, "Houses are in short supply and we don't want to find ourselves having to evict you. Sign this document."

It was a sworn statement that Judith and Agoak would not return unless they were legally married and had in their possession official testimony confirming this beyond any shadow of a doubt.

Once that was done, the bureaucrats went into a huddle and discussed in a half whisper whether Agoak should be tucked away in the White section or in the Eskimo village of Ikaluit. It was Agoak himself who cut short their discussions.

"I'm looking forward to working with Whites," he said, "but all the same I'd rather live in Ikaluit."

There were disapproving looks, but Agoak paid no attention. During his walking tours through Frobisher he had taken note of the freedom of movement enjoyed by the Inuit. They were allowed to go practically anywhere and, on the whole, to enjoy a degree of freedom Agoak had never witnessed before. He was aware that by moving into the Ikaluit neighborhood he might incur certain problems, but his idea of making the transition into White society involved a long, slow process, one which had begun for him quite some time ago. He was sixteen when, as a brilliant pupil at school, with little taste for hunting expeditions or meals of raw seal-meat or frozen fish, he had earned the right to complete his studies in Moosonee. Once there, however, and faced with the prospect of going to Toronto to take a university degree, he had hesitated, equivocated, weighed the alternatives and finally made his way back to Povungnituk. This was not necessarily the end of the matter, but for the time being there was Judith, whom he missed terribly. It had occurred to him to pluck her out of her present environment, bring her to Toronto with him and leave the Eskimo world behind them once and for all. But how could the two of them hope to survive in what was reputed to be such a hostile environment? Fearing the consequences of what he thought might be a rash undertaking, he had chosen to return, in the anticipation that there might be other paths to follow. And so he found work at the Co-operative, at the same time promising Judith that with prudence, foresight and diligence, he might manage to take her away with him one day.

Agoak spent much of that evening pondering his fate. With a cup of coffee on the table beside his armchair, he sat in his hotel room and passed his life in review. What struck him most of all was the felt presence of his primitive background. He conjured up childhood days when life was much as it was described in the ancient stories told by the old people. Naturally Agoak had not been born in an igloo; he had been raised in one of the prefabricated houses provided free for the Eskimos. His childhood home was an inelegant structure, a mere box, whose only saving grace seemed to be that it shut out the cold a little better than the traditional igloo. But there were three other children younger than Agoak in the house, with all the attendant noise, commotion and lack of privacy. Comforts which were now fairly commonplace had not always been available. Then one day electricity and propane gas had suddenly appeared, along with the snowmobile, which virtually replaced the dog-sled for winter travel. But the house was still small and they crowded together in it as best they could, and while the igloo seemed far off in the past, their present situation had little to commend it in the way of physical comfort. Agoak's father, whose talents as a sculptor quickly gained attention, earned a fairly good living at the Art Co-op, and the family allowance cheques from Ottawa helped too; but this only allowed them to escape abject poverty and nothing more. Agoak had long since resolved to realize his dreams and go elsewhere, go where an Inuk had the best prospects.

"One day I'll leave," Agoak had often said to Judith.

Judith, her face contorted and her eyes full of pain, would look away nervously. Usually she would say nothing, though occasionally she would mutter, "You'll never come back."

"I will come back, I promise."

Then she would begin to cry to herself.

Down through the ages, the Eskimo woman has played the role of the drudge, the slave, the subjugated but uncomplaining female. She has always been patient and resigned and since any thought of revolt would have made no sense in the community of people to which she belonged, in the end she experienced no feelings of real frustration. For one thing, she had no meaningful points of comparison. Eskimos who came into contact with Indians discovered living conditions pretty much the same as their own, except for those connected with the rigors of the climate. As for the women, they lived in the same subservience, and it was a matter of incontestable fact that in the old days, Agaguk's wife Iriook would never have seen this situation as cause for revolt.

Later on, everything changed. The Whites arrived and there was something new to contend with: women who were more independent, men who were more heedful. In those days the first contact with the Whites was a revelation for Iriook. For her, and others like her, nothing could be the same again. The seeds of revolt had been sown, with a minimum of fuss and flourish. Little by little the Eskimo woman learned to hold her own, to stop obeying her alleged master in so servile a fashion, and set about her work with less feeling of constraint or obligation. Life was hard, for her as well as her man, but she accepted this and gradually won more privileges, including a more equitable division of labor — this time in her favor.

The trouble was that some of the old attitudes were not so easily dispelled, nor was the Eskimo woman so easily liberated. Often times, even when in the right, she would choose to give in. Thus, Judith, though emancipated, educated and fairly uninhibited, tended to be meek and submissive with Agoak. Was this perhaps the form her love for him had taken? Perhaps she had unconsciously fashioned her behavior after the sort of white woman who, in her anxiety over the stability of a relationship, chooses to be submissive, at least as long as things remain uncertain. Agoak spoke of leaving and Judith could only cry.

In the end it was her only defence, a wholly instinctive and unreasoned way of taking refuge which she resorted to without knowing exactly why. With Agoak gone what would be left for her? A family of alcoholics who were drunk practically every night, fought among themselves at the slightest provocation and upset the whole village with the racket they made, while Judith's mother, an Eskimo of the old traditions, nursing the baby, closed her eyes and hummed quietly in a hoarse voice. . . . Was this her legacy, her future?

"I'll come back for you, I promise."

But Judith kept crying. Could she ever tell Agoak that her Uncle Josi had raped her one day? That her own father was always slipping his hand into her pants and fingering her while he asked: "Is it wet? Is it wet?" in the raspy voice of the incurable alcoholic.

She would have liked to leave as well, to get away from this houseful of whining brats, confirmed drunkards, hateful quarrels and perpetual poverty. All the different kinds of social insurance payments they received were barely enough to keep the men in alcohol. She was fairly well educated, but had no practical training, no trade, no skills. Thrown back on her resources, she had managed to get work as a domestic with some of the white residents of Povungnituk. Once, she had been hired at the Bay warehouse, because she was as strong and fit as a man. It was there that her uncle, taking advantage of an idle moment, had caught her by surprise and raped her on a pile of flour sacks. After this episode, which was fortunately never repeated, Judith was able to get herself hired in an English household. It was a job with little future, nothing to build ambitions on. But she had finally been noticed by Agoak, whom she had admired from afar ever since their school days. They saw each other once, then again, and little by little a bond developed between them and grew. Today they had progressed to the point of pondering their future together.

"I'll come back for you, I promise!" Agoak kept saying.

In Frobisher, going back was just what was on his mind. He was quite confident he could assimilate the banking routine quickly. There would be nothing too difficult or trying about his job, and the salary was more than sufficient. Even with the increased living costs and Judith to support, he would live well and be able to save some money. With his mind at ease, he could at last begin thinking about the much-promised journey back to Povungnituk to fetch Judith. Even if she did break down and cry this time, it was likely to be for reasons of sheer relief.

He already had a departure date in mind. Since it was now the beginning of August, there were only a few short weeks to wait until the Labor Day holiday in early September, when Agoak would have the time to make good on his promise. With the help of his savings, which he had hardly touched in these early days of his new life, he had gone ahead and reserved a charter plane, a solid Beaver transport, to take him to his beloved Judith.

Agoak's dream was a fine one and had been a long time in the making. For three years he had toiled to the limit of his talents, talents which, though raw at first, had gradually become more developed, more flexible, more marketable. In effect, he had had to start his education all over again from scratch, because what he had been taught in Moosonee was nothing more than a kind of key for the future. Little attention had been paid to the mysteries this key might one day unlock. Fortunately, when it came to penetrating the mysteries of modern accounting, he had the resources of a quick, bright mind to fall back on. The result was that after three years, he had acquired a self-confidence and a facility in handling problems which now gave him access to a position of responsibility. He was convinced that at the bank he would bring this same serene self-assurance to tasks no one yet dreamed him capable of. For only he was aware of the fact that he had undertaken a correspondence course in data processing and successfully mastered its intricacies, so that if the bank were ever linked up to a computer, he would not only be perfectly capable of operating the terminal but also of setting up the files and transferring the data into them.

It was infinitely more than anyone in that part of the country might have expected from a mere Eskimo. Agoak knew this and had cunningly revealed nothing more at the interview than his account-ing experience, which in itself was enough to get the job. One day he would be in a position to surprise the right person by displaying an expertise which had gone entirely unsuspected among his colleagues. Even Judith was not privy to the secret. As far as she was concerned, his rather disconcerting lack of availability several evenings a week had something to do with his studies, but just what kind of studies they were he had never revealed . . . any more than he had explained the reason for his stays in Montreal and Toronto, where he had gone for the purpose of logging twenty hours on a computer terminal and gaining practical experience as an operator.

He treasured his secret and it became for him a source of strength, like some vital wellspring. He had told the bank about nothing more than his basic skills and these had been found perfectly satisfactory. With what he held in reserve, any number of possibilities were open to him. As an Inuk descended from the age-old bands who had roamed the Arctic and managed to survive and reproduce, he was going to make his mark with characteristic poise and careful planning — but for once other than by hunting seal or bringing down the great white bear!

Yes, Agaguk seemed remote indeed, as did his world of icy misery and near-savagery!

CHAPTER II

Agoak was finally allocated a house in the Ikaluit area, which was inhabited almost exclusively by Eskimos. He had had the option of taking a house in Apex Hill, the point of highest elevation in the region, but there were few Eskimos living there. Agoak stuck to his original decision to live with Judith in Ikaluit, without being fully aware himself just how significant his gesture was.

The situation was paradoxical, as he knew perfectly well. Here he was, an Inuk with computer training and a qualified accountant, who chose to dress and eat like the Whites, who had long since abandoned Eskimo ways of thinking, here he was rejecting an opportunity to live among these same Whites, to enjoy their standard of living and many of the same amenities, all because of an instinctive decision which was as spontaneous as it was unfathomable. He had opted for a house which was definitely less luxurious — if one can speak of luxury in Frobisher — and of dubious construction, with its plywood walls, hemispheric roof and facilities which though adequate were more rudimentary than those of the houses in Apex Hill or the apartments in the town-centre complex. In fact, it was little better than a cabin, but Agoak felt somewhere inside that this was the choice he had to make.

Agoak had resolved while very young to extricate himself once and for all from the primitive conditions in which most of his people still lived. He had studied hard and applied all his intellectual resources to freeing himself from the grip of tradition. Not that he had ever felt any contempt for his ancestors. Although he had little sympathy for his grandfather Agaguk's primitive ways, he had nothing but admiration for his determined efforts to build a worthwhile life on his own terms. He had no less admiration for his grandmother Iriook,

9

since he recognized in her a unique quality which had allowed her to challenge nefarious and age-old customs, to the point of actually transforming Agaguk into a man sensitive to the most complex of human emotions. That was something he did not intend to forget.

But he was also aware of the dramatic changes which had gone on all around him. In Povungnituk he saw what Father Ricard's patient work as a social worker had achieved: a primitive people once barely capable of managing their own domestic affairs were suddenly taking on the formation of co-operatives, improving the quality of their lives and organizing the marketing of their sculptures, the product of an age-old art-form at once utilitarian and mythological. These ancient hunters of the whale, stalkers of the seal, "eaters of raw flesh" looked down upon by the Indians of the woodlands, had become administrators, officers of the Caisse Populaire, radio operators and, in keeping with the main local sources of livelihood, merchants and businessmen. It was still a far cry from the level of progress attained in Frobisher Bay, and Agoak was well aware of the fact, yet they were already very different from the igloo-dwellers who killed baby girls at birth and ate their own dogs in times of famine. Seeing an Eskimo from Povungnituk talking with perfect ease to a Co-op representative in Quebec City by HF radio, made one forget that less than a few decades before, this man's father thought nothing of eating a raw seal liver dripping with blood.

And yet Agoak, who had just cleared the last hurdle and might soon be enjoying all the benefits of life in the South, suddenly felt hesitant. He was proud and happy to have accomplished so much, but he was also worried that his forward motion had picked up so much momentum that he seemed prepared to abandon all the heroic generations in one sweeping gesture. This was why he had steered his course towards Ikaluit and decided to make it his base of operations in Frobisher.

What would Judith's reaction be? He would have to wait and see. Agoak had kept her in mind to some extent in making his choice. He had stalked around Frobisher and observed the behavior of the Eskimos who lived there. He had also noted the attitude of the Whites to the Inuit, as much as he could at least, and it was so different from Povungnituk, there was such an abyss between the situations in the two places, that he had been concerned not to make the transition too difficult for Judith.

This did not mean that racist attitudes were unknown in Povungnituk. In the final analysis the Whites are too powerful, and too unpredictable in their attitudes to the Eskimos, for the white inhabitants of POV (as it is known to the locals) to treat the native population in a uniformly forbearing way. Some even evince overt hostility. Judith had not therefore been able to avoid the occasional humiliating experience, but she had one thing in her favor: she lived among her own people, who were in the majority, she felt supported and sustained, and the damage done was usually not very serious. But in Frobisher, far from her loved ones, from familiar faces, from the familiar human and physical geography, how would she react to white hostility? Could she survive psychologically in a white community, cut off from daily contact with an Inuit community?

Agoak had often discussed the problems of race with Father Ricard. Ever since his stay in Toronto, where he had witnessed a kind of paternalistic and condescending racism, which is the hardest to contend with, Agoak had become aware of how difficult it was for an Inuk to find self-fulfilment in the Arctic. His discussions with Father Ricard had been fruitful and he had often tried to take them up again with Judith, in her own terms. Though she was intelligent and showed a surprising degree of adaptability, she was wracked with anxiety. She was afraid. She had once said to Agoak, "Aren't you afraid of venturing too far?"

The remark took him by surprise.

"I didn't know there were limits."

"Maybe there are."

"What do you mean?"

"You're moving into the White Man's world. Until now you've been able to set your own pace. But what if the Whites decided you'd gone far enough?"

"It's a free country, I'm a respectable citizen, I pay my taxes like everybody else, what reason could they have for deciding that?"

"I don't know, it's just a gut feeling I have."

Agoak did not attempt to pursue the point, but he had been left with a feeling of panic. For some time now, he had sensed the workings of powerful instincts in Judith. Far more than he, she seemed to have retained the sixth sense which for eons had been the Inuk's most valuable weapon and which explained better than any other single fact his near-miraculous ability to survive through tens of thousands of years in a climate which could only be described as cruel, destructive, implacable and relentless. Nevertheless, through living by his wits and with the help of the igloo, the harpoon, the dog-sled, clothing which warms with layers of air, fat to combat the cold, huge quantities of animal protein and direction finding by the stars, he had managed to survive and even multiply. As a result, he had no real need of the sophisticated tools the Whites brought with them when they first arrived. Naturally he did not hesitate to take advantage of them, especially metal goods, firearms, traps and, later on, snowmobiles. But he could have carried on as before, equipped with only the traditional resources, and probably survived longer than the Whites — and perhaps much better as well. Anyone familiar with the Arctic knows the construction problems caused by the permafrost, the year-round freeze-up of the soil which starts just below the surface and goes down 500 metres and more. He also knows that no tent, no temporary shelter of any kind, could ever match the igloo, which is quick to build, solid, comfortable, made from material which is available everywhere in unlimited quantities, costs nothing and can be left behind without the slightest regret, since at the next stopping point another one can be erected with just as little fuss. It was by placing unquestioning faith in instincts totally unknown to the White man that the Eskimo conquered the Arctic and managed to survive in it.

Judith, then, still possessed instincts which Agoak felt much less strongly. Having noticed this about her, he had found reason to be uneasy with her powers of perception. Though he may have been confident of success, of being able to blaze a trail for himself and go much further in life than the average Inuk, he still felt vague stirrings in his heart, stirrings which he would not even acknowledge, and it was as much to protect Judith as to prevent being uprooted himself that he had so unhesitatingly chosen to live in Ikaluit.

It was perhaps for these same reasons that he had avoided any premature discussions of his ambitions and plans. It was best that Judith learn her role as an assimilated, or near-assimilated, Eskimo woman, very gradually. And it was incumbent upon Agoak that he measure out the stages of this process with care and guide Judith along them wisely and patiently, for he was creating a life which she had never experienced before, or even dreamed of, and which she was certain to find baffling. Pursuing this apprenticeship in the midst of women of her own race and outlook was a more promising approach than flinging her into the hustle and bustle of Frobisher, where the rhythm of life was so very different from that in Povungnituk.

Saturday came and Agoak was finally free to take stock of all that had happened in this short time. He had left Povungnituk the Saturday before, in the early morning. He had slept in Chimo and spent Sunday there exploring the local resources, which disappointed him. On Monday he had boarded the Nordair flight and arrived in Frobisher Bay that same evening. And now, with the first week behind him, he had a job and a house, and a date was set for the charter flight on which he would go to POV to fetch Judith. That was a lot of water under the bridge; the first step, a giant step, had been taken, and Agoak was astonished that everything had fallen into place so easily.

This was the first free time he had had to himself since starting work, and during the night he had made a close examination of what he found around him. The house was scarcely better than the one he had had in Povungnituk, but it was better equipped. Bright and early, Agoak had gone on foot to the Bay to buy provisions, come back by taxi with all he had purchased and filled the refrigerator and cupboards. Then he had returned to the store, this time to get some furniture, a bed, a table and straight-back chairs, two armchairs, and a few lamps, as well as dishes, cutlery, and pots and pans.

By noon, having managed to locate a van to transport all his purchases instead of waiting for a store delivery, which would have meant postponing until the following week, Agoak found himself in a house equipped with all the necessities. There was even a little Japanese-made color TV sitting proudly on its gilt metal stand. With the Anik satellite now carrying broadcast signals as far north as compasses would function, the TV set would be their window on the world.

By evening, Agoak was well-ensconced in one of his new armchairs digesting the dinner he had prepared for himself in the sparkling white kitchen with the red curtains, using the propane gas cooker, which he continued to marvel at. It was a hefty appliance, worked by a number of buttons, with gauges, four burners and a big oven. Agoak had only seen two like it before, one at the home of the Hudson's Bay manager in POV, the other at the home of the Catholic missionary. And now he had one of his very own! Only yesterday he had been a mere bookkeeper; he had had nothing but his dreams. With one sweeping gesture, his whole life had taken on a new dimension. Was this not how it had been for Agaguk? In different circumstances, of course, determined by a primitive existence long since vanished, but similar in its basic form to what was happening today. When the old people told stories of an evening, they talked of how Agaguk had fled the village, how he had found a place to live of his own, then later returned to fetch Iriook, whom he took as his woman. They pooled their meagre resources and went to settle on the deserted tundra, toiling for decades to survive and bear children. And how Iriook, his woman, had managed to impart civilized ways to Agaguk, a new outlook which up to that point had been completely alien to him....

Was the course Agoak had set for himself, which had brought him here and led him to a new home, and which tomorrow would take him back to Povungnituk to get Judith Nooluk, was it so different? He had almost everything to offer this girl who was about to embark on a great journey with him, like Agaguk and Iriook before them.

CHAPTER III

Agoak discovered a whole new world at the bank as well. The manager was an anglophone White who had come all the way to the high Arctic harboring certain anxieties, although these had subsided with time, as he himself admitted, and he now seemed perfectly well-adjusted to the somewhat peculiar local problems of living, relating to people and conducting bank business. On the whole, banking transactions here are not all that different from those carried out in the South, apart from exceptional cases at least. But it is in connection with just such cases that there exist both problems and a sense of excitement, which together make banking in the Arctic unique. A loan to a seal hunter whose annual catch is virtually guaranteed has little in common with the kinds of loans usually extended in Montreal, Three Rivers or Kingston. It was a little unsettling to be dealing on a daily basis with Inuit who, having scarcely moved out of the Stone Age, seemed to navigate through credit transfers and term financing arrangements with as much self-assurance as they navigate kayaks through the treacherous waters and world-record tides of Frobisher Bay. Early in his tenure, the manager had had to muster an unusual degree of adaptability in order to cope with this unusual situation. It had not been easy for him, as he hinted to Agoak on the very first day.

"I intend to leave you with some pretty sizable responsibilities. I express myself poorly in Eskimo and I don't understand it very well either. You'll be doing the talking for me." He made it clear that he would play out a lot of rope to his new employee: it was up to him to see he did not hang himself with it.

Agoak was moved by this comment, and troubled too. He was comfortable enough with the intricacies of the banking business.

15

Perhaps he had begun in a special state of grace, with a calling. At the Caisse Populaire in POV, whose business involved more than just handling deposit accounts, he had quickly come to grips with the routines and procedures, and after his first few hours in a chartered bank he had seized on the similarities between the two systems, even though their respective terminologies differed in some ways.

At first the manager's remarks scared him a little, until he had examined their implications and came away not with a feeling of despair but with a carefully measured sense of anticipation. He was going to be given responsibilities in connection with the Eskimo clients, be made a kind of deacon for purposes of the financial rituals involved. He could scarcely have wished for more. From that day forward, he wore a broad smile of satisfaction. At the counter he was voluble and easy-going with the Inuit clients. He served them in their own language, and whenever he was presented with professional problems by his fellow Inuit, he broached them not only with the interests of the firm in mind, as was to be expected, but also, and to an equal extent, with the interests of the Eskimo in mind. He did not treat the Inuk like an anonymous file number but rather like a human being who had lived, as his ancestors had lived, in conditions of a difficulty the White Man had never known, and would never be capable of understanding. Agoak had been entrusted with duties which, within limits imposed by banking practice, would allow him to treat the Inuit with a kind of understanding they had seldom encountered before.

It was more than Agoak could have hoped for. It had occurred to him that in the long run he might arrive at a position of responsibility such as this; but he had never imagined that events would develop so quickly. He had even resigned himself to spending much longer actually looking for a job and had only vaguely expected to get taken on at the bank. Landing up there with so little effort seemed to him a sort of miracle. He had thought it much more likely that upon his arrival in Frobisher he would start by doing unskilled labor or servicing utilidors.* He had been assured that as an Eskimo with fluency in both Inuktitut and English, as well as a halting knowledge of French, he would have no trouble finding a job — though just what kind of job had not been specified. He had more readily

---

* Insulated tubes sitting above ground and enclosing water and sewage pipes, which service Northern settlements built on permafrost.

imagined himself working with his hands than being accepted straightaway as an employee of the bank. He had obviously had a stroke of luck walking in at the right moment. He would now do everything in his power to make sure he did not disappoint his superiors: he would devote himself to this job body and soul. It had become of paramount importance to him that he exemplify what an Eskimo could be when he put his mind to it and when others responded by placing their confidence in him. Agoak had a dream and in it he envisaged the development of close human and material commitments between the Inuit and the bank, commitments which he would initiate and one day, perhaps, orchestrate.

Agoak was walking on air. He harked back to his studies and the day when, conscious of the talent for mathematical reasoning he had always shown in his classes, he had decided to pursue this advantage as far as possible. Today, even though he regretted not having continued on into university, he realized that his expertise, which would be enriched by future practical experience at the bank and elsewhere, could take him further than an Eskimo had ever gone before.

All of this was enough to create a surge of euphoria in the pit of his stomach. Soon the urgent desire to share his high spirits with Judith became practically his only reason for living. He impatiently checked each day off the calendar until the Labor Day weekend, feeling beside himself at having to wait so long.

Finally the fated Saturday came, bringing with it the journey by chartered Beaver and the beginnings of the second phase of this adventure of a lifetime. Thus far, all the winning cards were in hand and a sunny future was on the horizon.

CHAPTER IV

Judith had now been in Frobisher two months. The snow, the ice, the bitter cold would be around until well into June, but the oil-fired central heating warmed the house nicely. Water simmered on the stove for much of the day, ready for making tea when needed. Judith had taken the time to hang some cheery, colorful pictures on the otherwise drab walls. Practically all day long a cassette recorder played quiet music which Judith listened to blissfully as she sewed or knitted.

One evening Agoak said, "If you want to get a job somewhere, you can."

Judith shook her head and smiled.

"Why?" she asked.

"As something for you to do, for your own enjoyment."

Judith, who had become his wife (for Agoak had quietly submitted to the regulation and got Father Ricard to marry them before they returned to Frobisher), got out of her armchair and snuggled up next to Agoak.

"Do we need the money?"

"No, not at all."

She kissed his neck, cooed, then took a thoughtful tone.

"I've got all I need here."

She pointed around the room, stopping as her finger reached the door.

"There's no drunkard coming in at all hours. The sounds a man makes don't scare me anymore."

"I know."

"Agoak, if you want me to work, I'll go and find a job."

"You're under no pressure."

"I'll certainly have a job one of these days, but I'd rather wait."

"As you like."

She climbed onto him, hot and quivering, and Agoak felt his own flesh swell, his penis ache with the urge to burst free. He took gentle hold of Judith, helped her to her feet, stood up himself and showed her the hard muscle which seemed as though it would rip open his pants.

Judith uttered a series of long, quiet groans in the back of her throat, pressed herself against him and moved her buttocks back and forth against Agoak's crotch. Then she spun around abruptly and threw herself against him in one movement, grinding her hips frantically as she cried, "Me too, me too . . ."

He led her into the bedroom and began to undress her feverishly. Beside Agoak's fairly trim frame, Judith seemed thick-set, almost chubby. Her hard breasts with their dark, swollen nipples were naked now and they excited Agoak, who began by softly caressing the very tips, pinching them and rubbing them with his palms. He then swallowed them voraciously, sucking them for all the pleasure they held, while his hands fondled the firm masses of flesh. Judith grimaced and rolled her eyes, as her hips moved back and forth in response to every throb in her vulva and vagina. Agoak quickly undid the fasteners of Judith's pants, which fell to the ground, and she lent a hand by pulling them off altogether. Then, while Agoak was getting his clothes off, Judith threw herself on the bed and rolled around on it fondling her breasts, her stomach, her vulva, moaning all the while.

After Agoak had tasted all her juices and brought on a series of orgasms by playing his tongue over Judith's vulva, he penetrated her at last and both let out long, gut-wrenching cries which became a single howl of pleasure when his sperm exploded into the woman's orgasm.

After two months, and a very gradual start, they had made considerable progress in their love-making. It was in this house, which they had moved into as man and wife, that their first act of love had taken place. Previously, in all the time they had spent together, they had restricted themselves to furtive kisses and fondling of breasts, although on one more auspicious occasion, Judith had slipped her hand into Agoak's pants and briefly caressed his penis, causing him to ejaculate. This so aroused Judith that even with so little stimulation, she was soon in the splendid throes of her first orgasm.

The great joy they shared that evening marked a turning point in their relationship. Agoak had been patient, gentle and understanding.

On a previous evening, the evening of their arrival in Frobisher, the long-awaited mutual exploration of their bodies was about to take the form of an attempt at penetration when Judith said, "You're hurting me. . . . I was all messed up by my uncle, go easy."

Agoak withdrew immediately. Later on, after long kisses and much fondling of her breasts, Agoak gently explored her vulva, and short of actually inserting his finger managed to summon an ardent response from Judith's clitoris with his skillful manipulations. For Agoak as much as for Judith, this was part of an initiation into sexual techniques which neither of them had reached by any natural progression. Both had read a number of sex manuals recommended — and in some cases actually provided — by a government nurse who happened to be travelling through their area; sometimes, when they were able to find a little peace and quiet, they would read them together. They were therefore applying from memory caresses learned beforehand, caresses fondly hoped for but till then unrealized.

"I'll be patient," said Agoak the evening he had tried to enter her. "We've got our whole lives in front of us."

Judith in her gratitude had then attended to Agoak's pleasure. At first she had only caressed his penis with her hands. Later, over the days and weeks of their apprenticeship, as Agoak had inspired orgasm with his lips and tongue, so too Judith took to bringing the fleshy penis to her mouth and quickly learned how to trigger an ejaculation.

They tried penetration, which was still painful for a while, then became easier as their attempts continued. To finish with they would come back to their caressing, their oral love-making, in a state of greater and greater abandon. The soaking wet sheets and sweating bodies bore witness to the intensity of their passion. Every evening the house rang with their cries. Then there was a kind of slack period when they both seemed to need to recover their composure and contented themselves with affectionate gestures and terse conversations, Eskimo style. Agoak would relate the highlights of his busy day, while Judith talked about the more limited demands made on her as a housewife who lived alone, without children, in a house which was relatively easy to maintain.

When they began to talk of the future, the tone changed a little. "You know," said Agoak, "I'm gaining ground every day at the bank."

"What do you mean?"

"I'm taking on more and more responsibilities."

"The bank lets you?"

"I wouldn't take them on if it didn't."

"Will you become manager some day?"

That was a weighty question; Agoak thought it over before answering.

"One day, yes, I might."

"When the English leaves?"

"Or I'm posted somewhere else."

That evening the wind was strong, unpredictable, close to the ground. The walls of the house trembled occasionally in the impertinent gusts.

"Somewhere else?"

"Yes."

"With the Inuit, like here?"

"Perhaps."

"What do you mean — perhaps?"

"It might be farther away."

"In the South?"

"Yes."

"With the Whites?"

There was so much despair in Judith's voice that Agoak felt a sudden reluctance to continue.

He got up and switched on their color TV. It was eight o'clock Monday evening and in Frobisher it was time to watch the adventures of *Cannon.* Judith methodically laid her knitting to one side and said to Agoak, "We'll need to talk more about this."

Then, with her man beside her, she became engrossed in the action on the screen.

Two days later, they finally reached their ultimate erotic goal and then every evening for a good week they did their best to recreate what they had discovered — a completely fulfilling experience, an absolute and utter sense of mutual abandon. For the moment Agoak's obsession with future plans were forgotten. Their sexual destiny had taken them so far, and they were capable of attaining such extraordinary heights of pleasure, that nothing else seemed to matter.

Often in the course of the day Agoak was forced to do violence to his feelings in order to recover some measure of lost concentration. But his other dreams, his personal dreams of career and future, were not forgotten completely. As sexual experimentation lost its novelty, its urgency, the day in fact came when Agoak's daydreaming turned sharply away from conjugal bliss to the more distant future. The day also came, after a certain amount of procrastination, when Judith decided to pay a little less attention to the life of pleasure and begin pondering the remarks made by her husband on the subject of work.

An old Eskimo woman who lived nearby had developed an interest in Judith from the moment the young woman had moved into the Ikaluit house. She said her name was Kuksuk and that she was a grandmother who lived alone on an old-age pension and a pension granted her as the widow of an Inuk who had long worked at utilidor maintenance and garbage collection. Kuksuk knew that some day soon she would be sent to the golden-age home people talked about, which housed Inuit past their prime. In earlier times, tribal law required that these old people be left to die, for they were just so many useless mouths to feed and had to be eliminated. They could choose the means of death, but they could not postpone it. An igloo was built for the old person and he was left in it without fire, lamp or provisions to die alone of cold and starvation. This was the iron law of tradition. Today, this ancient and barbaric custom has been superseded and old people are crammed into dull, lifeless buildings — which happen to be well heated and stocked with food. But there is more than one way to die of starvation. Before long Kuksuk would be taken from her home and forced to finish her days as best she could in an institution built to house the useless members of society.

She had communicated all this to Judith with the short, pithy sentences of an old Inuk not much given to verbosity. She was a remnant of the ancient tribes, all wizened and toothless. One day long ago her husband had brought her to Frobisher, where he had immediately found work. The woman Kuksuk could have been had since reached old age, and in a particularly distasteful manner, as she pointed out.

"I live like a White woman. I lived in an igloo, then here," she continued. "I loved the igloo. I was young and strong."

She flexed her arm muscles.

"I kept strong because I worked hard."

Judith had heard other old women tell the story of their youth. The work they did was usually taxing, work fit for beasts of burden. There were not only the daily chores in the igloo, which in themselves were not too demanding. The man often needed help outdoors as well, which meant strapping the children on to the sled and carrying the baby in the hood of the anorak, running along on snowshoes, helping the dogs pull their load, as well as watching out for seal, like a man, shooting like a man too, and no mercy if the shot was wide of the mark, confronting polar bears, and if by chance a kill was made, gutting, skinning and butchering the seal or the walrus or the caribou or the one-ton polar bear. Horrendous tasks which could overwhelm and exhaust even young men in their prime, and which the women faced unflinchingly.

"But I stayed strong," concluded Kuksuk.

She feigned a desperate look and rocked from side to side whining, "Ha-Ya-Ha-Yah, look at me."

She touched the leathery skin on her naked, emaciated arms, which stuck out of the openings in her sweater. She took off the sweater to reveal her breasts, droopy, flaccid sacks which had lost all their flesh and turned a horrible brownish color, with nipples shrivelled up like raisins. She uncovered Judith's firm breasts and fondled and caressed them as she sighed with admiration.

"I was once like you," she said, "beautiful and solid. But I live in this White man's house and look at me. It makes me sad."

"But why?" asked Judith. "You're comfortable there."

"I'm dying. You're dying too."

"I don't understand," said Judith.

"When I went with my husband," continued Kuksuk, "I was alive. He came here, he worked, but he worked alone. I was left in this house. I began to die. And time finishes you off."

"But I'm happy," said Judith.

"Can you work with him, at his bank, and share his tasks? And while you're at home, what do you do with your arms, your muscles, your strength?"

This was the longest sentence Kuksuk had ever uttered in Judith's presence. The young woman was nonplussed. She looked at this unsightly creature with her slobbery mouth, who chewed tobacco and spat where she liked: she had lived life to the full, but was much the worse for it now. Would Judith also be emaciated and decrepit like this one day?

Judith could not get Kuksuk's words out of her mind. She knew perfectly well she could not lend Agoak a helping hand at the bank. She could not, in her ignorance, even discuss his work with him in the evening. Being alone in the house and still childless, she could say all there was to say about her working day, such as it was, in no time at all. She could hardly dwell for long on the fact that she had made the bed, mopped, dusted, done some dishes and put dinner on to cook, especially in a house where everything practically ran itself, with central heating, hot running water and even snow removal taken care of.

What to do about all this? Perhaps Kuksuk was right. Perhaps this kind of progress was just another way to a slow death.

One morning Judith could contain herself no longer and instead of letting her visit to Kuksuk revolve around the usual cups of tea and humdrum conversation, she arrived at the old woman's home determined to seek out advice. She came straight to the point.

"Agoak wants much more out of life," she said.

"Here?"

"Not necessarily. He talks of going somewhere else."

"To where the Whites are, in the big cities of the South?"

"Yes, I suppose so."

"I've seen pictures, the ones that move."

"Films and television."

"Yes. I've seen all that. It's very shiny and very dry. There doesn't seem to be any wind or any snow."

"They have snow in the South too."

"But it's all soft and sticky. Suastsiok has been there. When he came back he told us all about it. He was sick. The air down there looks clear, but it's dirty, there's something invisible in it that eats away your stomach."

"I know," said Judith. "Agoak went to Toronto and he said the snow was dirty."

"The air too."

"Yes, the air too."

"You see?"

"I know," said Judith sadly.

"He wants to go there?"

"Agoak says there's no limit to what he can do. He might even be manager of a bank some day."

"And will you be with him?"

"Yes."

"Somewhere where there's nothing but Whites?"

"Probably."

"There are Whites here too," said the old woman. "They're big and strong, their houses are tall and bright. They go up and down the streets in their cars and snowmobiles, and their planes make a big racket as they pass over our heads. But we Inuit are strong in numbers.

The Whites had to give us houses, they greet us in the street, they let us go anywhere, they don't make life too difficult for us, our children go to their schools. Here everything is fine."

"And?"

"But what is there in the South?"

"Whites, like here."

"And that's all there is — Whites!" said Kuksuk in a contemptuous tone. She spat out a brown gob of tobacco juice and punctuated her gesture with an Eskimo expletive.

"E-E-E-Ea."

Then she took her head in her hands and swayed around as she moaned, "Ah-ya . . . why does Agoak have an *agiortok** in his head? A man who listens to an evil spirit is doomed."

Suddenly the old woman broke into a smile. She stretched her hands out in front of her, palms forward, "An Inuk always remains an Inuk," she said. "You must not forget that. He should remember that too."

More upset than ever, Judith returned home and spent what seemed to her a very long day.

That evening, after dinner, she led Agoak to the sofa, sat him down and snuggled up next to him.

"Talk to me," she said.

Agoak looked surprised. Judith's request was not unusual in itself, but there was a tone in her voice which was. Agoak seemed in a quandary, wondering what was up.

"Talk to me," Judith repeated.

"Do you have something to say to me?" asked Agoak.

She shrugged her shoulders, "I just want to hear your voice," she said.

Agoak smiled.

"I get the feeling you have something on your mind," he said quietly.

Judith bit her lip, thought for a moment, then suddenly made a resolve. She gestured around the room, indicating the furniture, the TV set . . .

"Where's all this leading, Agoak?"

He looked at her with an inscrutable expression.

"What are you driving at?"

Judith threw up both hands in a vaguely imploring gesture, "Agoak, you've talked about going to live in other places."

---

* Evil spirit.

"Yes."

"Of maybe leaving."

"Ah, I see, and you're frightened by the prospect?"

She hesitated, then shook her head, "Not really frightened, but ..."

"But ...?"

"But going to live with the Whites?"

"Wherever it's necessary," said Agoak, who then asked, "Have you been seeing a lot of old Kuksuk?"

"Not every day."

"No?"

"No."

"But you've been seeing her."

"Yes."

"You have talks with her."

"Yes."

"You've told her I want to leave?"

"I've said you mentioned it, yes."

"I've talked about it as a possibility. Did you explain that?"

"Not ... not really."

Agoak was patient. He put his arm around her shoulders.

"Kuksuk is old," he said. "Sometimes old people are wise and it's worth pausing over what they have to say about things. At other times, it's not."

"You don't think she's always wise?"

"When it comes to the modern world, the one we live in, the world of the Whites, even our own, a woman like Kuksuk understands nothing."

"Some of what she says is true."

"Oh?"

"That the snow in Toronto is dirty. You told me that yourself."

"Yes."

"The air's dirty too and eats away your stomach."

Agoak got up. He stood in front of Judith and talked very quietly in a patient, understanding tone, the way he had talked to her before in her time of distress, in Povungnituk, when she had been overcome by feelings of panic.

"You spend too much time alone. The only company you've found is with an old woman who wants to destroy you. I should've known something like this would happen."

He paced up and down the room, then found his words, "I think you should find a job outside the house."

"What about our meals?"

"We'll manage. Being all alone is putting ideas in your head."
Judith lowered her eyes and murmured, "You want me to work?"
Agoak began to say something, but caught himself.

"Will you need the money I earn?" Judith continued.

Agoak had never revealed the amount of his weekly salary to
Judith, in the belief it could not be of any interest to his wife. She took
no part in the financial management of the household and depended
on him for everything.

He nodded: he had a trick up his sleeve. He just might have found a
solution to Judith's lonely anxieties, a way to force her to move in
step with him along the roads he wished to travel. He was in effect
telling a lie by not letting Judith know that his salary was quite
sufficient and that she could just as well stay home. But if she did, it
would only be to worry herself sick with fear and delusions.

"Yes, I will need it."

Judith nervously took hold of Agoak's arm, "Is it too expensive
living here?"

"No, no, you don't understand."

"But you just said it would help if I was earning a salary."

"We could save more, have a better life, go out more often."

"I like being at home with you when you're not at work."

"We should get out and meet people, make friends."

"I don't need to meet people and I don't want any friends."

"But I have to get to know some people and move around more in
Frobisher, for my work. Having friends is important."

Judith looked away, then shrugged her shoulders, "Fine, I'll go
and work if you say so."

"Yes, I'm saying so."

"But I don't have an education like you. Where am I going to find
work?"

"Do you remember eating with me in the hotel coffee shop?"

"Yes."

"Yesterday I heard them saying they were looking for one or two
girls to wait on tables. You could do that."

"When we were there the place was full of girls serving. Have they
all disappeared?"

"They were students earning money before heading back to the
South."

They went to bed early that evening and there was little love-
making. Agoak fell asleep quickly but Judith lay awake for a good
while staring into the dark. Agoak was certainly right: it was best she

found something to busy herself with. It wasn't good for her to be idle. But could Agoak appreciate the great peace, the relief Judith felt at having been rescued from her family at last? Naturally she still had anxious moments, but that could never compare to the brawling, the carousing, the obscenities, the beatings, the crying fits which never seemed to cease, which were the stuff of her daily life in Povungnituk. At last she was in a secure, peaceful environment surrounded by her own things. She had been wrong to get so upset and especially to bring Agoak into it. Suddenly, in the silence of the night with nothing outside but the distant and barely perceptible buzzing of snowmobiles, Judith had a horrible thought. In a flurry of panic she woke Agoak from a sound sleep. He came to in a daze, his heart beating wildly.

"What is it?"

"What if I'm working, Agoak, and I have a child one day, what will I do?"

"You'll stay home with him, of course."

Judith smiled happily in the dark. She felt reassured. She had also stumbled on an unexpectedly rapid solution to her dilemma.

"Agoak," she murmured, "make me a child . . ."

He chuckled softly and made affectionate noises, then undressed Judith by feel, got undressed himself and let his fingers, hands and mouth roam over his wife's body, causing the tension to build up in her muscles and nerves while Judith did the same thing to Agoak's body. Soon the sheet was soaking wet, and Judith's desperate moans prompted the final union, the knotting of their flesh in a last contorsive spasm, the ultimate cry of completion. She then fell into a deep sleep, with her belly full of sperm, while Agoak, who had collapsed against her, fell into a deep sleep devoid of thoughts or dreams.

In Judith's moist, intimate recesses a minute creature made its way in the direction of the waiting ovum. The next day it would reach its goal, effect its penetration, so that in due course a child would be born to Judith.

CHAPTER V

Agoak secured Judith the job he had talked about without her having to lift a finger. The people who ran the hotel were customers of the bank. Agoak knew them and often had occasion to talk with the manager of the coffee shop on his breaks. They knew Judith by sight and they respected Agoak. Since Judith was attractive, well-groomed and polite, they willingly agreed to make her a waitress, despite her lack of any practical experience in that line of work. Agoak assured them that his Judith was bright and resourceful, that she learned quickly and would create no problems for them. The very next morning she was at her post by seven o'clock. And since she had been unable to serve Agoak his usual breakfast at the house, she served it to him instead at the coffee shop. This was to become a regular routine for them every weekday for some time to come.

"You'll see," said Judith to her husband with a giggle, "Sunday mornings when I don't have to be at work, I'll make a breakfast fit for a king and bring it to you in bed."

Agoak had not been wrong in recommending Judith to the people at the hotel. By Friday, after barely five days, she had become a waitress the manager could describe as one of the nicest and most able he had ever hired.

"If only she was a bit less shy . . .," he said.

"As far as I can tell," said Agoak, "that's something that'll never change. She's always been that way and always will be."

"Listen, I'm not making that a condition," added the manager, "I'm quite happy with her as she is."

At the house that evening, Agoak was touched when he saw how happy Judith was.

"You were right," she said, "you were right, Agoak. I enjoy my work, I feel good there. People are so nice to me."

31

"Even the Whites?" asked Agoak a little pointedly.

"Yes, even the Whites." Then, embarrassed at having to admit it, she added, "Especially the Whites."

Life went on, but now everything had changed. Judith was up early in the morning in order to rush off to work. Agoak slept a little longer, got up at his appointed time, made himself a coffee which he drank as he washed up, then around eight o'clock arrived at the coffee shop, where it was Judith's privilege to serve him. At noon Agoak came in for a light meal, served him of course by Judith. She finished at three o'clock, returned home and fixed dinner for Agoak, who was off work at five. Two or three evenings a week they went to a movie or to the bowling alley, or got together with people at one of the recreational centres.

Then, one Sunday evening, they opened their door to their first guests, a white couple, an employee of the Territorial government and his wife.

It was a relaxed, pleasant evening. The wife was a regular at the coffee shop and already knew Judith. The husband had often had dealings with Agoak at the bank and they had got to know each other, man to man. By the time their guests left, around midnight, the beginnings of a friendship were already evident. They saw one another again the following Sunday, at the home of the white couple, in Apex Hill. Their relationship followed its natural course, each couple, from one time to the next, discovering in the other certain affinities and mutual sympathies. Like Agoak, the other man was ambitious, and his career was already well under way. Like Judith, his wife worked outside the home, as an employee of the telephone company, and since both of them served the public, they had a shared experience which brought them closer together.

Later on, an Eskimo couple came and joined the four of them. The other Eskimo, like Agoak, had a substantial education and spoke perfect English, as did his wife. Nochasak worked at the airport. A little older than his new-found friends, he had a son in Toronto who was already a pilot. His son's dream was one day to take command of the Nordair jet which flew the regular service to Montreal. When he had logged enough hours working as a co-pilot for a smaller airline and became eligible for a job with Nordair, he intended to do everything within his power to get himself hired. Meanwhile, he was taking night courses in order to learn about all the different guidance systems and was getting practical training on some of the systems in use in Canadian and American airports.

Judith listened dreamily as her Eskimo guests talked about their child's future. And as their other friend talked nonchalantly about plans that were many years in the future — all to a chorus of agreement from his wife. Yes, they too would have children. And he explained what he wanted for them.

"We'll return to the South and they'll go to the best schools, no matter what. I'd like my son to be a doctor some day, or an engineer . . ."

Everybody had their say. Nochasak had another son and two daughters.

"I'm saving my money," he said. "When the time comes, we'll be able to send them off to study anything, anywhere, even if it costs thousands and thousands of dollars."

"I want my children to have the best in life," said Judith with a dreamy look in her eyes.

"But what do you want them to become?" asked Nochasak's wife. "What is the best in life anyway?"

"Whatever they choose to be, on their own."

"Children still need some guidance," interjected the White woman.

"They'll choose their own fate," replied Judith.

"And what if they chose to remain igloo-Eskimos all their lives?" asked Nochasak abruptly.

"If that made them happy," replied Judith, "more power to them."

Sensing that she had ventured onto thin ice, she blushed deeply and got up with an awkward motion, making a sort of pirouette.

"Let's move to the table," she exclaimed. "I'll make some coffee and I've got a cake I baked myself. Come on!"

Life had certainly changed for Judith and Agoak. Judith, for her part, had not been back to see Kuksuk for weeks. The old woman and her forecasts of gloom and doom were now the furthest thing from Judith's mind. She had virtually forgotten all that had been said and she realized she was no longer in the grip of the same paralyzing fear. She still had an occasional pang when she left work and went into the bank for a moment to say hello to her husband, which she would do if he wasn't too busy. Whenever she saw him in his handsome ready-made suit, with a nice shirt and a well-knotted tie, she felt a little shudder. It seemed to her that this man bore no resemblance to the Agoak she had known in Povungnituk. In fact it seemed to her that he even bore little resemblance to an Eskimo any more. Something subtle, intangible, made him seem more and more like a White.

On one occasion Judith left in a hurry and tossed off some remark about being late, which was nothing more than a convenient excuse invented on the spur of the moment. She went home and took a while to calm down. Then she began to think to herself how crazy it was for her to act that way. The two of them were happy, and what she took to be a White man's demeanor in Agoak was simply a manifestation of his success, his happiness, of the satisfaction he derived from doing his job well, from being respected and admired.

When Agoak arrived back at the end of the day, dinner was on the table. It was good, for it had been prepared with love, and Judith, who had finally calmed down, had nothing but a pretty smile and kind words for her man.

Two weeks went by and one afternoon, just after Judith got home, Kuksuk came knocking on her door.

"You don't come," she said, "so I come."

"I'm working now," Judith replied, "so I'm not here during the day anymore."

"I know. You work for the Whites, you work with the Whites."

"Yes."

"And you invite Whites over here."

"I also invite Nochasak!"

"Some Inuit are more white than the Whites. They're traitors, they don't deserve to live!"

The old woman was slobbering and staring aggressively at Judith with her rheumy eyes.

"Why are you looking at me like that? Why are you saying these things?"

"Are you becoming White too?"

Judith lost her patience at that point.

"If Agoak was here he'd throw you out!"

"Who's Agoak?"

"You know perfectly well!"

"You mean the man who sleeps in your bed every night?"

"Don't talk like that!"

Judith could imagine what the old woman was about to say and had no desire to hear it.

"That man's no Inuk," said Kuksuk in a falsetto voice, "he's a White. You sleep with a White, you'll have a White man's children."

"Shut up!" Judith yelled. "I don't want to hear any more!"

Just then Agoak came in and spotted the old woman, hunched over, leaning on her cane, a skeletal and sinister figure.

He took Kuksuk by the arm and led her gently outside, then all the way to her own door two houses away, while she yelled at him in a voice trembling with rage, "Let go of me, you dirty White! You're no Inuk! Agiortok! Traitor! Liar!"

When he got back, Agoak collapsed in an armchair and remained silent for a while. Judith was leaning against the wall by a window sobbing hysterically, unable to collect herself, her stomach knotted with pain.

Finally, through her tears she said, "Why do people think you're a traitor?"

"People?"

"Kuksuk."

"People are one thing — the ravings of a crazy old woman, that's something else."

"She may be old, but she's not crazy."

"So you're prepared to listen to her, are you?"

"No, in fact I was in the middle of telling her that if you were here, you'd throw her out."

"But now you're all upset and defending her."

Judith extended her hands and with an imploring look said, "Agoak, help me, I don't understand anything anymore!" Agoak sighed and shook his head slowly, "What is it you don't understand? We're comfortable here, aren't we? We're happy, aren't we? We have a good life, you like your work. . . . Do you like your work?"

"Yes, of course."

"We have some close friends, we go out, we talk with people, we socialize, we belong in this town. . . ."

"Do we really belong in it?"

"Has anyone ever insulted you or even given you the cold shoulder?"

"No."

"Do our friends respect you?"

"Yes."

"People in Frobisher, your boss, the customers, the other waitresses, don't they all respect you?"

"Yes, yes!"

"Same thing for me at the bank. Don't you find that an important consideration? Is that how things were in Povungnituk?"

"No, not always."

"Add up all the Whites there are. Six times, ten times, a hundred times more than there were in POV, and we're living well, we're relaxed, happy, fulfilled."

"But what about in the South?"

"It's not so different."

"I've heard there's discrimination."

"There is. There is everywhere. Even here, if you looked hard enough you'd find it. But it's directed mainly against Inuit who don't know how to behave, who can't hold their liquor, who are lazy or dishonest. It's the same in the South. Is that the kind of Inuit we are?"

"No."

"We're punctual, responsible, we work hard. Look at Nochasak. He's the same way. He has grown children who are doing well in the South. Don't you find that encouraging?"

Judith had stopped answering. Her head was lowered in a reflective pose.

"Am I right about all this, Judith?" asked Agoak.

"Kuksuk kept shouting you were a traitor."

Agoak burst out laughing, "Are you still worried about what she said?"

Judith walked slowly over to the window, her face impassive, her shoulders thrust back. Suddenly she seemed to stiffen, gave a wave of the hand and called over Agoak in a peremptory tone, "Come here."

Agoak walked over to her side. Judith pointed through the window.

"Look," she said.

The scene was a familiar one: an Eskimo, his wife (who was carrying a baby in her hood) and two older children, were leading two sleds, each of which was pulled along by a team of six dogs. They had come south-east, ultimately no doubt from the Brevoort Islands on the inland arm of the Cumberland Sea, now that the ice was setting in again. They were all in snowshoes, adults and children, the sleds were heavily laden and everyone was doing his best to urge on the dogs, who were unaccustomed to built-up areas and were becoming more and more skittish as the group advanced.

Agoak and Judith contemplated the scene in silence.

"They've had a long journey," said Agoak finally.

"Yes," said Judith, "I guess they've come to trade some skins and get some provisions. Now, do those children look sturdy?"

"What are you driving at?"

She pointed to the man.

"You aren't like him anymore."

"Obviously I'm not."

"You haven't been for a long time."

"I know."

"How many like him are left?"

"Oh, I don't know, a few thousand."

"And what do they have, compared to what you have?"

"If they live near a town, like this one, or some other good-sized settlement, they'll have access to a variety of provisions, they'll have medical care and the government's help in surviving. And if they live right in the settlement or town, their children will go to school."

"A white school?"

"Of course."

"Of course, because there aren't any others."

She frowned.

"Do *you* help them?" she asked.

"At the bank? When I can, but it's not easy. They're always on the move, especially if they live on the islands or further up, towards Clyde or near the Cumberland Sea."

"And apart from the bank?"

"I don't see what you mean."

"When you put on your three-piece suit from the Bay, or walk around in your synthetic fur coat and snowmobile boots with the yellow trim, what are you doing for them?"

"What do you expect me to do? The social welfare agencies and the RCMP look after them. What can I do all by myself?"

"Don't you feel you're betraying them? Aren't you a traitor?"

Agoak, flushed with anger, was almost shouting.

"Because I don't live like them, like a savage?"

Judith shrugged her shoulders, walked pensively around the kitchen, then decided to put on her boots and anorak.

"Are you going out?" asked Agoak.

"Yes. Dinner's on the stove. You can just help yourself. You're a White, so you shouldn't have any trouble playing housewife!"

"Are you going to Kuksuk's?"

Judith brushed off the question with a sweep of her chin and walked out.

Through the glass in the door Agoak could see her heading for the hotel complex and the coffee shop. He assumed she was going to have a coffee and talk with people there. He walked back into the centre of the room and stood there for a while staring into space. Then he got out a cup, poured himself some tea and sat down at the table. He drank the scalding beverage in small, careful sips.

They had just experienced their first quarrel. But was it really a quarrel? Agoak did not entirely understand what Judith was getting at. He failed to understand her reasoning. His own behavior seemed perfectly rational to him. He had freely chosen to better his lot, to escape the bonds of the primitive life, and Judith had known that all along. He recalled that she had often given him encouragement and consoled him when things weren't going as he wished. She had seemed very pleased about his coming to Frobisher and happy about going back with him. Now she seemed to have reversed her position. What did she want? Did she actually want him to revert to the traditional Eskimo life again? Did she have any idea of the work that entailed for her, the unrelenting hardships, which meant spending most of the day just trying to survive? Wasn't she happy working in clean surroundings, prettily dressed in her fetching uniform, her sleek hair piled up in a bun, all the while surrounded by smiles and pleasant manners? Would she rather brave the fury of the Arctic, choosing a miserable existence instead of a comfortable, well-organized one? Here there was the magic of electricity and central heating, and thanks to the utilidors, which were impervious to the worst cold, the most inclement weather, there was also running water and sewage disposal. Life was good in this house, as it was in the big complex in the centre of town. Did she want to jettison all that, along with their whole future, the chance to get ahead, the exciting possibilities open to both them and their children? . . . It was a logic Agoak simply couldn't understand. Why, after moving so far along the road to success, should he now shift into reverse? And what was behind this business of helping his fellow Eskimos? The best way to help was to prove to the Whites through his own achievements that an Inuk could go far in life and do so with grace and skill, if given half a chance. Even the Inuk he had just seen leading the dog-sleds — could he not, given the opportunity, realize his potential just as well as Agoak? And his children too, perhaps even more so than he.

But first you had to feel strongly about leaving this land of ice and snow and unspeakable cold. You had to look beyond the horizon, towards the land of milk and honey. You had to use your brain and your powers of reasoning for some purpose other than overcoming a thousand and one dangers just to secure a miserable bit of raw meat or fish or frozen whale blubber, which was often too tough to chew . . . all this in order to stave off the threat of death, until the day might come when there was nothing left of the Inuk and his family but a few frozen corpses lost forever somewhere on the icy Arctic wastes.

It seemed to Agoak to be tempting fate, to say nothing of good fortune, to deprive oneself of such an agreeable opportunity to gain access to a better life and a better world, and to excel in ways few would think possible for an Inuk.

In the old days, the endless winter nights in the igloos were often spent improvising long epic songs which gave an immortality of sorts to the many Inuit deemed to be the bravest, most skillful hunters and fishermen, the elite of the miraculous harpoon. Was it not within the realm of possibility that, at some future time, they would be singing the praises of other skills, of other successes, of other achievements? They had sung Agaguk's praises. Now they could sing Agoak's as well, if for different reasons.

The more Agoak pondered all this, the less able he was to understand what might be troubling Judith. He had imagined that being alone in the house was putting misguided ideas into her head; he had therefore persuaded her to take a job. Judith had plunged enthusiastically into her work. She seemed relaxed and happy and was living her life to the full. Yet it had needed nothing more than a spiteful visit from old Kuksuk and the inopportune arrival of a family of primitive Eskimos in order for the same anxieties suddenly to take hold of Judith again. Did it take so little to upset everything? Were yesterday's fears and misgivings still that close to the surface?

And to top it all off, she had actually criticized him for the way he dressed!

Agoak really had no idea any more what to think about this strange turn of events. Judith was apparently angry as she left the house earlier. But had he confused anger with distress? Was it spite or sorrow that had her so upset? Or both? Agoak's entire education, after all, had been based on figures, and a mind trained in this way often has little grasp of the subtleties of human behavior. What he was confronted with now was no mere problem of financial accounting, but one of emotional and, it might be said, even sociological accounting. Naturally he was aware of the sort of intolerant reception he might encounter at a later stage in his career. But he had calculated the risks which might be in store with an almost mathematical precision. He realized that he had a most effective weapon in his calm, confident mastery of certain skills and that his skills could only grow with time. Provided he consolidated them and made good use of them, what had he to fear? He could not understand why Judith seemed incapable of using what she had learned in order to grasp something he thought was perfectly logical. What did it matter if they did set out for the cities in the South? He would have more to distinguish him than his brown skin and flat features: he would also have his invaluable experience and acknowledged expertise.

Agoak, lost in his thoughts, had not kept track of the time. The minutes had been ticking away, however, and when he finally glanced at the clock, he was surprised to see it was already nine and that Judith was still not back. Outside it was a peaceful evening, and the lights from centre-town sparkled in the snow piled up in front of the house. Agoak wondered what to do: there wasn't a sign of Judith. Should he be getting worried about her? Should he make the first move? She was unlikely to be encountering any trouble, that much he knew. At the same time, he was curious to know where she was. In the end he knew very little of what went on in her head. How could he expect to predict her actions? It occurred to him that she might have done something rash. But what? Judith was introverted. She had never shown herself capable of violence or even an angry outburst. Today she had probably reached the limits of any selfish streak she might have. Was she capable of anything worse? Agoak had trouble believing so. And yet, the thought suddenly struck him — did he really know his wife? He made up his mind. It took only a moment for him to dress; he left the house and headed at a brisk pace towards the imposing silhouette of the hotel building.

Agoak did not have to look for long. Judith was sitting in the coffee shop with an Inuit couple and their two children. He recognized them immediately as the family they had seen passing by the house with their dog-sleds as they arrived from somewhere far away.

Judith spotted Agoak and got up without waiting for him to reach their table. She dressed in the twinkling of an eye and walked straight over to her husband. He was barely as far as the cash register when Judith accosted him. The Eskimo couple watched the scene impassively from three tables away.

"I'm ready to leave," said Judith.

Agoak started to walk towards the other couple, but Judith took him by the arm and pushed him gently through the entrance-way.

"Come on," she said, "we're going home."

Once outside, Agoak stopped. He shook his head slowly.

"I don't understand," he said.

"What?"

"Don't you want me to talk to your new friends? Who are they? Where are they from?"

Judith shrugged her shoulders and walked off quickly in the direction of the house. Agoak tried to keep up with her, but she managed to stay several steps ahead of him. Judith got back first and didn't stop until she reached the kitchen table.

"Well, are you going to answer me?" asked Agoak.

He got undressed slowly. Judith just stood there with her outdoor clothes on, staring defiantly at her husband.

"Why should I?"

"Because I believe I asked you a perfectly legitimate question."

"Really?"

"Yes, Judith. Back there it seemed as if you didn't want me to talk to your friends."

"Maybe I didn't."

"Why?"

"Maybe they wouldn't have understood you."

"I'm an Inuk, like them. I speak Inuktitut, like them. You know that perfectly well."

"Yes, I know that, but there's more to it than just language. . . ."

"What, for example?"

"What you say with the language, what you talk about."

"Am I supposed to be worried about that?"

"Yes."

"You'd better explain yourself."

"They're Inuit, those people, real Inuit. There weren't any like them even in Povungnituk."

"I spotted them right away. . . ."

"Real Inuit?"

"Yes."

"That's what you said, is it?"

"Yes."

"So I'm not a real Inuk then?" asked Agoak calmly.

"No, not like they are."

"And I wouldn't have understood them?"

"Worse still, they wouldn't have understood you."

"Oh really?"

"They have the same word for living as you, but it doesn't mean the same thing for them."

"You're talking nonsense!"

"No. For you, living means being a White. For them, it means being an Inuk. That's how big the difference is."

"Did they talk about themselves?"

"Yes."

"About the misery, the occasional famine, the cold, the back-breaking work, the endless journeys on snowshoes?"

"Yes."

"About how savage an existence it is!"

"No!"

"Are you going to stand there and deny it? Look around you. Do you think they don't envy you? If that woman saw your house, do you think she'd be happy to return to her igloo?"

"She doesn't want to have anything to do with my house."

"Is that what she told you?"

"Yes."

"So you'd like to live like them, would you?"

"I'm not sure."

"You're not serious!"

"All I'm saying is I'm not sure."

"And this woman told you she wanted nothing to do with your house? She actually said that?"

"Yes!"

"I presume they live in an igloo."

"And in a tent during the summer."

"I'll ask you once more: would you like to live like them, wandering from one place to another according to how good the hunting is, bringing up children without any chance to go to school?"

Judith lowered her head and fell silent. Agoak had never seen such an expression of consternation on her face. He was about to walk over and take her in his arms when she darted away, taking off her anorak as she went. She went into the bedroom without uttering a sound. Agoak stood motionless, rooted to the spot. He heard her in the darkened room taking off her boots, undressing and, then when everything was quiet, going to bed. He sat down in an armchair, lit a cigarette and waited till she fell asleep. Only later did he realize he hadn't eaten and that supper was simmering on the stove. He went and shut off the burner, then sat down again. It was past midnight when he finally went to bed himself.

In the middle of the night, something woke him up which he couldn't identify at first. After a moment he realized Judith was crying. He came to and turned towards her. In a voice broken by sobs, she said, "Agoak, I think I'm going crazy. I don't know what I'm saying anymore. Forgive me. You're good and I love you."

"Go to sleep," breathed Agoak, "get some rest."

He held her tightly in his arms. In the warmth of his embrace she was soon asleep.

In the morning, which had come up grey with a thick, enveloping snowfall, Agoak could not help but think that something serious had happened the night before, something which would affect them both for a long time to come. Yet he was still unable to discern what the cause, or the implications, of this experience might be. However, since Judith was all smiles when he came in to the coffee shop for his breakfast, he decided to respond in kind and smiled back.

CHAPTER VI

Strangely enough, Judith seemed to return to her old ways in the weeks that followed. There were a few days when the atmosphere was awkward, if not really tense, when she had fewer smiles to offer and was more withdrawn than usual, but Agoak had decided not to let on about anything, to be as attentive and concerned as ever and in particular to let nothing, whether by word or deed, whether sympathetic or impatient, act as a reminder of the exchange they had had, which Agoak now thought of as a moment of madness. And yet, he should have seen it coming. Judith had never really been enthusiastic about their new life. He had long known that his wife feared the White man's world. He had never imagined that she would react so strongly, but it was better, in any case, to let things lie for the moment and just wait. Judith had to do some thinking on her own. The night of their argument she had actually asked Agoak to forgive her. She had acknowledged her distress and tacitly confessed to being in the wrong. It wasn't much to go on, yet it was reassuring, for here was proof that Judith was grappling with the problem. It was even possible that the smiles and the return to a happy sex life, full of untold heights of pleasure, might signify a return to common sense. Agoak, in any case, clung to this hope in order to drive out the unpleasant memories — without, however, putting more stock by it than was called for. He was beginning to understand how certain men could find women complicated and unpredictable, not to say unstable. Was Agoak up against a real change of heart or nothing more than irrational behavior? He concluded that only time would tell and that meanwhile it was best to keep quiet on the subject.

It was also best that they live as normally as possible. If Judith was willing to carry on with her daily duties, as though nothing had happened, fine, that was tolerable. And one day perhaps the bubble would break. For the time being, his work at the bank demanded all of Agoak's energies. Judith, too, had her responsibilities. She had to work hard, but her tips were good and the bank account she had opened on her husband's advice was growing steadily.

Once or twice she had asked Agoak, "Do you need money? I've already saved several hundred dollars of my own, which you can have if you like."

But Agoak declined.

"I might need it one of these days, but everything's fine for the moment. Keep saving, you're off to a good start."

As their respective tasks took on unforeseen dimensions, they gave more and more of themselves. They continued to receive people at home and make new friends. Their free time was now taken up with a variety of activities, bowling, social get-togethers, shows, snow-mobile excursions into the surrounding countryside. If Kuksuk were to have come back to Agoak's she would find the door closed. She and Judith had had no new confrontations; nor had she and Agoak, an even less likely eventuality. This was perhaps the one thing that was guaranteed to keep the couple on good terms. Other Inuit who lived the traditional life turned up in Frobisher from time to time, and Agoak would see the odd one come in to the bank to do business or the coffee shop to have a bite to eat. He and Judith might meet up with some on a Saturday or Sunday, but nothing untoward happened when they did. Judith carried on as if she had not even seen them and she said nothing more about the family she had talked with in the coffee shop. Agoak, of course, kept mum. A truce was therefore established which, in Agoak's estimation, might be either long- or short-lived. Or even permanent, who could say?

Thus the weeks went by, without any reminder of the near-disaster they had lived through. One morning as he arrived at work an hour before the doors of the bank opened, Agoak was called to the manager's office.

There was nothing unusual about this, for the day often began with a review and assessment of the previous day's business. Agoak therefore walked into his boss's office feeling quite relaxed. However, the man behind the desk had a long face. Agoak stood watching him in silence. Whenever he had seen this expression before, it always signalled serious trouble. Yet Agoak was quite confident he had done nothing irregular. In the preceding few days, in fact, business had been so routine, predictable and easy to handle, that the manager was more likely to be suffering from boredom than anxiety.

"Sit down," he said to Agoak, pointing to the chair in front of him. Feeling easy in his mind yet a little concerned, Agoak sat down.

"I've got some unpleasant news for you."

Agoak broke into a cold sweat.

"It's something I just hadn't anticipated for the near future. Believe me, I didn't hire you knowing this would happen. I expected I'd be breaking you into the work here, then if necessary, sending you off for further training. . . . Anyway, things have turned out differently, much to my regret. You're one of the best employees I've had in a long time."

Agoak sat motionless, his mouth dry. He suddenly realized he was about to be dismissed. With some difficulty he managed to ask, "What . . . what's going on?"

The manager sighed and threw up his hands.

"I've known for two days now and haven't been able to get around to telling you. We'll soon be linked up to a computer at the head office in Montreal. They can do it now with the Anik satellite. . . . Wait a minute, you seem to find this funny."

Agoak was leaning forward and chuckling to himself.

"You're laughing? I'm giving you your notice and you're laughing?"

"Tell me," said Agoak, "did they describe the system to you?"

"What system?"

"I doubt very much it's COBOL. Given the way our data is organized here, I wonder what it might be. Emulator? And what kind of operating system is that likely to be? 1400? DOS/VS, DL/I, CICS/VS? Didn't they give you any details?"

"I haven't the faintest idea what you're talking about."

"They didn't even tell you what computer language we'll be using? I might be able to figure out the operating system from that."

Agoak's astonished boss looked at him with his mouth open and his eyes as wide as saucers.

"Do you know about computers?"

"Of course."

"But you never let on."

"Let's just say I wanted to be able to surprise you one of these days."

"But where did you learn? Surely not at the Povungnituk Co-op."

"No. I took a correspondence course, then gave myself some time off to go to Montreal and Toronto in order to get practical experience on a terminal, with key-punching and the different job-control languages currently in use."

"You know all about that?"

"Of course."

"You mean if we had a terminal here, you could operate it?"

"Yes. And transfer our files to the central processor and access any data that was needed."

Agoak had never seen his boss so moved. Here he was, the cool, contained English-Canadian of good background, so non-plussed he was unable to contain himself. He got up, paced around the room, rubbed his hands together, laughed and finally walked over and touched Agoak on the shoulder.

"You're sure you know what you're talking about?"

He had hardly been able to believe his ears.

"Of course I am."

"All this stuff about operating systems and accessing . . . how does it go? . . ."

"Accessing data."

"Anyway, all this computer business is pretty much of a mystery to me. I was convinced I'd have to get someone in, I'd have to ask head office to send me a man."

With a burst of enthusiasm he exclaimed, "That's the best damned joke I've heard yet. I have the man right here. I had him all the time!"

The manager had never been so exuberant about anything.

"I'd never have believed it!" he said. "Not in a million years!"

Agoak was overcome by his boss's infectious good spirits and he too was now laughing and briskly rubbing his hands together.

"You should have told me," said the manager. "Why didn't you tell me, in fact?"

"I was waiting for the right moment," replied Agoak. "Like this one."

The manager opened the cupboard near his desk and took out a bottle and two glasses.

"We must drink to that. This calls for a celebration."

"I'm sorry," said Agoak, "but it's too early in the morning, I couldn't."

"A computer expert!" exclaimed the manager. "And sober as a judge to boot. I must be doing something right!"

Agoak recovered his composure and asked, "When might you know what operating system and language are involved? I'm going to have to do a little brushing up, at least a few hours' worth, especially if they're using a Honeywell 58, since I never had much chance to familiarize myself with it."

"I've got an idea," said the manager. "I'll fill in for you at the counter when we open, while you make yourself comfortable here and telephone the data-processing unit at the head office in Montreal."

"Maybe that would be the easiest way to go about it."

"You can tell them all they need to know about the amount of space we have here, the electric current and I don't know what all else."

"Okay."

"Go ahead and call them. It's ten o'clock and time for us to open, but you just take as long as you need."

Alone now, Agoak pulled a pad of paper towards him and began dialing the Montreal number. Seeing how happy his boss had been to learn he was not going to lose his teller, warmed Agoak's heart. He had always felt appreciated at the bank, but in the steady rhythm of his day-to-day work, Agoak's conversations with his superior were always couched in the impersonal language of the banker. For the first time ever, his boss had gone beyond simple approval and given free rein to emotions Agoak had not thought him capable of. He had also underlined more explicitly and categorically than he had ever done before just how much he valued his employee.

Agoak was flabbergasted. He hadn't anticipated all this in his wildest dreams. Although he had long felt ready to participate fully in North American life, he had not, until this morning, had any tangible proof of his eligibility. Now that he had such proof, he felt capable of climbing to dizzying heights of success.

A voice answered in Montreal.

"Hello," said Agoak in a calm, self-assured tone. "Give me the head of data-processing, please."

That morning Agoak skipped his break and didn't go to the coffee shop until his usual lunch-time. The place was so jammed that the waitresses were barely keeping up with the orders. But there must have been something unusual written on his face, because Judith managed to get over to him almost immediately.

"I'll just have something light today," he said.

"I won't be able to serve you right away. Do you mind waiting a little while?"

"Okay, but . . ."

Judith leaned over and said: "I came over to find out if there was something going on. You look like a different person!"

"No, there's nothing going on."

She turned on her heel and went to look after some customers by the window who were clamoring for service. But she looked back at

Agoak twice, as if she were genuinely puzzled by what she had seen. Agoak had made a resolution on his way to lunch. The fact was that throughout this memorable morning he had been haunted by the question of Judith's possible reaction. Six months earlier Agoak would have announced the good news without a second thought. But ever since the onset of Judith's strange behavior in the past few weeks, she had said enough (more than enough!) about her real feelings to serve, if not exactly as a basis for discussion, certainly as a warning to Agoak. What he had to tell Judith would certainly not strike the same responsive chord in her as it had in his boss. There was suddenly something inexorable about Agoak's ambition to explore new worlds. How would Judith react? In Agoak's estimation, the gossip that would soon be circulating about him among his wife's friends, from one end to another of this isolated little town, would serve to soften the initial blow, and Agoak would therefore have an easier time explaining himself.

But it had not occurred to him that so much would show on his face. Should he tell Judith everything that evening? And look for some sort of miracle in the meantime? But what exactly would he say to Judith if no excuse came along before closing?

Agoak got his miracle, even if it was less than earth-shaking and fairly predictable. At four o'clock that afternoon, the manager called Agoak into his office again.

"I've been talking to Montreal myself," he said. "They sounded pretty pleased with what you seem to know about computers. I asked for and got you a raise, effective next pay day."

The amount involved was substantial, in fact surprising. Agoak could now boast that he was comfortably within the White man's salary range. He no longer had to think of himself as a man of color, who was paid a pittance and treated condescendingly. This was the piece of news he could report unhesitatingly to Judith that very evening, and which he could rely on to explain the expression he had been wearing at lunch-time.

He soon discovered, however, that he was not the only one bearing good tidings. No sooner had he made Judith aware of his success at the office than she announced in turn, "I've had some news today myself. I didn't talk to you about it before because I wanted to be sure. The hospital telephoned me this afternoon with my test results."

"What test results?"

"They were positive. I'm pregnant!"

It was a strange evening. Agoak had been bowled over by the news of Judith's pregnancy. It was too much for one day. Too much sheer

joy. Their cup was filled to overflowing, a new day had dawned in
their lives and they now had entirely too much good fortune to
contend with. He almost wanted to go and bang his head against the
wall or pinch himself, to be sure he wasn't dreaming. It hardly seemed
possible that all this could sweep over them at once, like a beneficent
tide, a great wave of happiness. He sat smiling in his armchair with
his hands folded together on his lap, his ears buzzing, his heart racing
and his brain full of sweet music.

"I'd like to telephone my friends and tell them the news," said
Judith at one point.

Agoak sat up with a start. A professionally ingrained prudence
suddenly came to the fore.

"About my raise?"

"No," said Judith, in a reproving tone. "It's up to you to say what
you want about that. I was talking about the little fellow I'm carrying
inside me."

"Of course," said Agoak, relieved. "Tell anybody you like. And
speaking of the little fellow, keep in mind that it could just as well be
a little girl."

Judith giggled in an uncharacteristically mischievous tone.

"Or both, Agoak," she said, "and maybe even more. Can't you just
see me having three or four babies all at once?"

"Stop!" exclaimed Agoak. "I'd need a raise three times bigger than
what I got. I mean can you see us with four cradles lined up in the
bedroom?"

"And can you imagine the anorak I'd need, with a hood big enough
for four?"

Agoak's face fell.

"Do you plan to carry the baby in your hood?"

"Certainly."

"The traditional way . . ."

"Yes!"

Agoak was seized with an overwhelming urge to tell Judith
everything. To let her know that he would be handling the computer,
that he had just moved up considerably in the ranks, that nothing
would be the same for them again. He wanted to blurt out to her that
as the wife of the most important employee of the bank after the
manager, she had no need to wear traditional clothing and could
indulge herself in the smartest fashions. He was well aware, however,
that his argument would carry little weight. Most of the White
women in Frobisher wore an anorak and there were as many White
babies swaying about in hoods as there were Eskimo babies. So too

for mukluks: the only people without them were Whites from the South, who went around in their conventional city boots. It did not take long, however, before the average visitor went to the store to buy himself a pair of these very practical and comfortable snow-boots. In the final analysis, just about everybody wore mukluks and anoraks . . . and had an infant nestled in their hood!

How, then was he to present his case in a convincing way?

His momentary panic over, Agoak began to recover his composure. He felt childish for having had such silly, even fatuous thoughts. Why should his professional accomplishments exercise any influence over the way Judith dressed in a remote town, where everybody had to conduct themselves and even think in much the same manner, since it was the climate that counted, rather than social rank or any citizen's alleged importance. In Montreal or Toronto it would be important — and certainly much easier — to act and dress according to certain social standards, because everything would be different — climate, attitudes, responsibilities, personal relations. But here?

Judith chattered away and buzzed around the house like a woman possessed. Agoak had never heard her talk so long and loud and make so little sense. It was striking to see such a concentration of happiness, an all-embracing force that took hold of the whole being. What struck Agoak most was the luminous quality of Judith's smile. There was a feeling of joy he had never known her to experience before. This served to restore his peace of mind, and for the time being at least, he stopped worrying about the possible impact any rumors about his promotion at the bank might have on Judith in the days to come.

Settled in his armchair with the perpetual cup of hot tea in his hand, Agoak contemplated Judith's noisy and restless mood of elation. It was a sight to behold, something Agoak could never have imagined. Judith was a new woman, with new and unsuspected facets of herself to reveal. She was behaving so differently that once or twice the thought briefly crossed Agoak's mind that the woman standing before him was not Judith at all but someone who was a complete stranger to him.

However the couple's real discoveries that evening took place in bed. Judith had been so beside herself with joy when making dinner that she had burned it and so they had ended up eating sandwiches. Agoak opened a bottle of wine which they sipped slowly while they talked about the child who was on the way . . . except that poor Agoak, who was still being the gracious listener, could hardly get a word in edge-wise, since Judith had become so talkative.

When at last they were drunk with both wine and happiness and decided to go to bed, Agoak did not have to exercise any initiative. That evening it was Judith who had her clothes off first, hurrying Agoak along, helping him undress faster, pulling him impatiently into bed, pouncing on him immediately, taking him as he would take her, drawing out his desires, nibbling him, sniffing at him, swallowing his penis and then his sperm, beginning the arousal all over again, despite Agoak's pleadings, masturbating as she sucked his joy, trembling with a series of intense orgasms, until the moment came when she straddled her male, forced him into her and brought them to one last, powerful simultaneous orgasm. And throughout this display of unbridled passion Judith whispered, murmured, sighed and moaned the same refrain, "Thank you!   Thank you!   Thank you!"

Morning came and had the courtesy not to be dull and overcast. During the night high winds had dispersed the clouds and the result, despite the polar cold, was a clear day with a captivating quality of unreality which left a ridge of gold along the horizon.

Agoak felt a great sense of relief as he stood at the window waiting to go to work. He was, as usual, all alone in the house, since Judith was already on duty at the coffee shop. This reddish-gold line at the horizon, this horizon towards which he was headed on a pretty well clear path, felt almost symbolic and he could hardly avert his glance from it.

It was a peaceful moment. Agoak thought to himself that Judith now had a source of happiness all her own, like a bright, bubbly spring at which to slake her thirst.

At work Agoak discovered that his wife's pregnancy was the news of the day among the Eskimo women on the staff. Even the manager seemed to be in on it, because he gestured to Agoak through the glass partition in his office by putting his hands together and shaking them back and forth, in the signal for victory. Later he came over to whisper congratulations in his ear, and it then occurred to Agoak that if this piece of news had already travelled so far so fast, the one about the computer, and his role in its operation, would not take long to make the rounds either.

Any doubts disappeared with the arrival of his first English customers. All of them wore a proud expression as they congratulated Agoak — not, this time, over Judith's pregnancy, but over the business of the computer terminal.

Yes, news certainly did travel fast in Frobisher. But then that was the fate of remote cities, cut off from civilization, like Schefferville, Labrador City, Fermont and so many others: it was almost impossible to keep a secret in any of them. People of all different sorts are thrown together on a daily basis, while sensational events are few and far between, so that the merest rumor can take on headline proportions. As with Judith's pregnancy and Agoak's sudden promotion.

When he walked into the coffee shop on his break, Agoak knew that even at this early juncture, Judith already knew everything. She strode right over to him the moment he sat down in one of the booths. Agoak detected a strange mixture of contentment and anxiety on her face. Before she could open her mouth, Agoak asked her, "How do you feel this morning?"

The note of concern in his voice appeared to disarm Judith. She laughed softly and shook her head in a coquettish way.

"Look at me," she said smiling, "how do you think I feel?"

"Happy," said Agoak.

"You're right, that's exactly how I feel — happy. I feel as if I'm wearing a protective shield of happiness around me, like a suit of armor."

Though the waitresses were not supposed to do so, Judith sat down in the booth beside her husband.

"I hear you're something of a computer expert."

"Only on the terminal, at the tail end of the process."

"The what?"

"I'll explain all that later. So you've heard the news, have you?"

"Yes. And I felt like an idiot. I didn't know what people were talking about. Why didn't you let me know sooner?"

Agoak looked away and wondered how best to answer her question, without going into details. He was conscious of the time and of the responsibilities that awaited them both. His reply came in a calm, measured voice, though one which gave hints of a new-found and largely untested strength of will.

"What I tried to accomplish," he said, "I wanted to accomplish in secret, to make it a big surprise. I wanted to prove something and I had to do it alone, without any outside help."

"And what was it you wanted to prove?"

"What an Inuk can do if given the chance."

Judith sat for a while staring at the floor and thinking. Then she looked Agoak right in the eyes and said in a somewhat brusque tone, "You mean how easily an Inuk can become a White if he wants to?"

She got up and left. She came back with her husband's coffee, put it on the table and left again before Agoak, who had one finger in the air, could get out what he was on the verge of saying.

For Agoak, the rest of the day brought a mixture of varied emotions, a kind of bizarre and cacophonous rhapsody which ran from euphoria to remorse. The man had been through the whole emotional gamut in the last two days. Unfortunately, the positive experiences were not quite enough to outweigh the negative ones. Agoak felt an abyss opening up between him and Judith, in spite of the fact he was confident of having acted with the best of motives. As far as he was concerned, he had nothing to reproach himself for. Say what she might, Judith would never convince him he was some sort of traitor for having wanted to improve his lot in life, escape from the dire conditions of his childhood, move up the ladder of success. What had all that got to do with being a traitor? Father Ricard himself had endorsed Agoak's plans and testified as to their soundness. Could a man whose family still lived in conditions of unimaginable physical misery, without any realistic hope for the future, be blamed for wanting to improve his lot and rise above conditions no human being should be compelled to tolerate?

If he had been successful, it was certainly not at his family's expense. They had not been asked to make any sacrifices for his sake. It was by working in the summer and saving his money that Agoak paid for the privilege of going away to school. Though the government covered certain educational costs for Eskimos at all levels of schooling, this still left other expenses for the student to pay. Agoak had made certain his father was never obliged to pay these expenses for him. He had earned every necessary dollar himself and didn't owe anything to anybody, least of all his family.

And now he was being treated like a leper, a pariah, for having ambitions he saw as absolutely justifiable.

How he would have liked to be in Povungnituk just at that moment, sitting and discussing the problem with Father Ricard — and perhaps entrusting him with the task of persuading Judith to take a different stand on things! But here in Frobisher, whom could he approach? Whom would Judith be prepared to listen to? Who might manage to make her see the light? Not one of the people who came to mind fulfilled the basic condition: not being White, at least not the sort of White who was typical of the majority in Frobisher. There weren't, after all, twenty Father Ricards in all the world. Agoak might have gone so far as to say that there was only one. Judith just might accept advice from him; she certainly wouldn't from anyone else. There seemed to be no solution . . . unless of course they were to go to Povungnituk.

Agoak worked through his day as best he could. There had been some problems at the counter for a while which had kept him absorbed. Later on he had received some telexes from Montreal concerning the computer link and he had had to study these and begin drafting his reply.

When he got home he was too tired to take offence at Judith's less than enthusiastic welcome. He ate in silence, then went to his armchair and turned on the TV. Later, much later, when the news was over and it was time for bed, he said to Judith in a non-committal tone, "How would you like to go to Povungnituk one of these days?"

"Did you want to see your family?"

"For one thing."

"I've got no desire to see mine."

Agoak was about to say: 'Why not? — they're Eskimos who live the traditional life, drinking, brawling, stealing . . .', but he restrained himself and just nodded his head. Judith cleared away their cups, locked the doors and was about to turn out the lights, when she suddenly turned to Agoak and said, "You want me to have a talk with Father Ricard, don't you . . .?"

Astonished by Judith's perspicacity, Agoak stared at her coldly, "And what if I do?"

"What would be the point?"

Agoak waved his hand vaguely in the air and replied, "To try to make you understand some things I think he can explain better than I can."

"I understand perfectly well," said Judith. "In fact, I understand too well. I don't need his explanations. I haven't made any declarations of war, so don't go looking for targets to shoot at."

They left it at that, since even though Agoak had wanted to have the whole thing out, Judith hadn't left him the chance to do so. When he walked into the bedroom, she was already in bed with her back turned to him. He stood there for a moment wondering if he should say anything more, but as she wasn't budging, he went to bed as well. A little while later he leaned over and whispered to the back of her neck, "Judith . . ."

She jerked impatiently and said, "I've got a hard day's work waiting for me tomorrow, and so do you. Let's be sensible and get some sleep."

Agoak debated for a moment as to whether he should re-open the discussion, but decided that Judith was right, she had to get up early to be at work by seven, and he had plenty to do himself, especially with the new arrangements at the bank. He fell into a troubled sleep, his mind assailed by nightmares.

The next morning, with Judith already gone, Agoak slowly sipped his coffee as he sat at the kitchen table. Everything seemed to be getting more complicated by the hour; every happy piece of news brought something unpleasant in its wake. A certain thought came welling up in Agoak's mind as he recalled the conversation they had had one evening with their White friends and Nochasak.

Judith seemed to have been saying that she would leave her children free to make their own decisions about the future. Did this mean she would let them return to the ancient Inuit way of life if they wished to do so? And wouldn't this, more than anything, more than ever, create an unbridgeable gap between him and his wife?

Agoak, sitting alone with his coffee, had never felt less happy. He thought back to when he was first seeing Judith and to their attempts at reaching a mutual understanding. It had taken months before they were really talking. As he mulled this over, Agoak suddenly realized that he had often talked at length about his future plans, but had hardly ever heard an opinion on the subject from Judith, no words of encouragement, certainly nothing like positive enthusiastic support. Something more like polite and neutral silence.

As he set off for work, his mind was a whirl of confusion over how to deal with Judith. He felt helpless and sick at heart. His idea of taking her to see Father Ricard and trying to fire up her enthusiasm had already met with a miserable defeat. She had seen through his ploy and from now on she would be suspicious. If there was another way to look at the issue, or someone else who could help, Agoak was unable to see what, or who, this might be. The worst thing of all was that Judith had never really explained how she felt about all this. She had said some pretty harsh things, she had accused Agoak of treachery, she had made some murky claims about his doing nothing to help the most underprivileged Inuit — but she had never made it clear what form this help might take. The truth was, as Agoak had to admit, that up till then their arguments had been based more on emotion than anything else. Judith had expressed her fears, but had not attempted to understand them. She put a lot of stock in gut reactions, but refused to discuss the facts. It was inconceivable to Agoak that she would refuse to acknowledge that they were well-off now and had a rosy future in store. It seemed equally inconceivable that she could have more or less admitted to a longing for the nomadic life in igloo and tent, for the precarious sort of existence led by

Inuit who could not, or would not, take advantage of the progress achieved in the Arctic. True, the progress in question was the work of the White man, but since for the moment this was more than the Inuit were capable of, was it not best to take advantage of what was being offered? And at the same time build up an Eskimo society which would eventually assume a new role in partnership with White society, and create opportunities for the Inuk to enjoy well-being, respect and access to the whole world, if his needs and tastes so dictated? . . .

Agoak had never yet managed to put this vision of things into words. He was pretty sure, moreover, that Judith would never hear him out if he attempted to do so. Agoak was still completely baffled as to why. His whole being, with its stake in mathematical precision, rebelled at the idea that a formula for life as clear as his could be so thoroughly misunderstood and in fact rejected out of hand by Judith.

As he walked into the bank, Agoak had an idea. He had suddenly thought of someone who might know how to handle a discussion with Judith. Agoak was resigned to the fact that he was never going to make Judith listen. Someone who might manage it, however, was Nochasak. It was worth a try, at least.

He worked away and felt a little better. Like a drowning man who tries to save himself by clutching at flotsam, Agoak clung to the idea that Nochasak would succeed where he had failed.

He skipped his coffee-break and decided against sending an explanation to Judith with a teller who was on her way to the coffee shop. He telephoned the airport, where Nochasak worked, and announced he was coming out to eat with him at the canteen. He asked the bank manager to give him some extra time off at lunch, and when twelve o'clock sounded he headed off for his appointment with Nochasak in the Nanook taxi.

His fellow Inuk was surprised.

"I thought you ate in the place Judith works at," he said.

"Things are different today," replied Agoak. "I can safely say that things are different today."

They ordered their meals, and when the young waitress was gone, Agoak looked Nochasak right in the eye.

"I need your help," he said.

"I'll do what I can, count on it. Oh, I almost forgot to congratulate you. Judith called my wife. You're expecting a child. That's fantastic! I hope for you it's a boy."

"I'll take what comes," said Agoak. "Anyway, thank you . . ."

Nochasak watched him fidget for a moment, then finally, to help him get started, said, "You've got problems, I gather."

"Yes, I must confess, I do."

"It can't be money."

"No."

"In fact I also learned you gave your boss quite a shock at the bank."

"Yes."

"Something to do with computers."

"That's right."

"It's always nice," said Nochasak, "when an Inuk can make a White sit up and take notice like that. . . . So what about these problems?"

"Something's been going on, and I've got two ideas I'd like to try out."

"First things first: what's been going on?"

"It's Judith."

"Oh?"

"Nochasak, have you noticed anything lately?"

"No, nothing in particular."

Then he added discreetly, "It all depends what you want to know."

"Judith doesn't approve of my having a career."

"What?"

"What I mean is, a career in the White world. Sometimes I wonder if she wouldn't like to see me become a nomad."

"The two of you together?"

"That's the idea."

"And the children you may have?" pursued Nochasak. "Like the ancient Eskimos?"

"Exactly."

Nochasak weighed his words carefully, "My wife and I hadn't guessed it in exactly those terms, but we had noticed that Judith stays pretty quiet whenever you talk about your future plans. There was one occasion when she seemed to be in a rage because you were speaking well of your boss. It was no big deal, it happened one minute and was gone the next. But we did begin to wonder."

"I've begun to wonder too and all the answers I come up with have me scared."

"She wants both of you to go back to the traditional life?"

"Nochasak, I just don't know. I can't manage to get her into a real discussion, the kind of thing where we could speak our minds and get it over with once and for all."

"It's crazy," said Nochasak. "A couple having a falling out like that so soon after getting married."

"And it's no little falling out," said Agoak. "Believe me, it's serious."

"I thought she was happy about being pregnant."

"She is, and it's beautiful to see. But at the same time I know she's terribly unhappy."

"Because of your promotion at the bank?"

"Yes, among other things."

"She must be pleased, with the salary. . . ."

"From what I can tell, she's afraid we might go and live in the South, in a big city."

"Might you?"

Agoak thought before answering.

"I've worked hard since the age of sixteen to get where I am," he said. "I don't like the idea of having to put limits on my ambition and depriving myself of the chance to finish what I started."

"I understand."

"If finishing what I started means ending up in Toronto, why should I stay stuck in Frobisher or any place like it?"

"Personally," said Nochasak, "I've never wanted to leave here."

"Why not?"

"Because of my wife, perhaps. She has the same fears about the South. She's always said this was the perfect town for us. It's got stores, people, electricity, running water, well-paid jobs. Going elsewhere, we'd lose what we have here."

"That sounds like Judith's line of reasoning, if I understood it correctly."

"Well?"

"I can't stay stuck here. I've got my sights aimed higher, much higher."

"Have you explained all this to Judith?"

Agoak didn't answer. Instead he asked Nochasak, "Has your wife ever called you a traitor?"

"No."

"Mine has."

"That's strange. Did she elaborate?"

"That's the trouble, I don't know what she thinks or what she wants. Sometimes I get the feeling she'd really like to live the ancient life, running behind a dog-sled, eating raw meat in the igloo. . . . But at other times, I don't know, I just don't know."

"She wouldn't like to go and live in Toronto, for example?"

"I don't think so."

"Neither would my wife," said Nochasak.

Agoak was no longer sure whether he had done the right thing in asking for Nochasak's help.

"Have you ever thought of going to live in Toronto or somewhere?" he asked his friend.

"Yes, I have."

"Would you have gone out of necessity, to improve your lot, really make something of your life?"

"When I was younger, yes. I would have liked to work in the control tower at the airport here, and end up working at Dorval or Malton or even in the States."

"Would you have gone against your wife's wishes?"

"I wouldn't have gone alone."

"What if she hadn't wanted to go with you?"

"I would've stayed."

"Does that mean that's what I should do? Is that what you'd advise?"

"No. First of all, everyone has his own life, his own story, his own motives, his way of seeing things. Another thing: I was just a laborer. I'm a foreman today, but I had no special training. I was strong, I liked working, I was always punctual, and I had no desire to lead a nomadic life. I wasn't a man with special skills, like you, able to speak two languages."

"Almost three," interjected Agoak. "I won't have any trouble perfecting my French."

"Fine. Which means you could do great things if you left. That's different. On the other hand, if you stay here, with the pile of skills you have, and Frobisher pushes ahead just a little, you could carve out a nice future for yourself."

"I know," said Agoak, "but I want to feel free to choose exactly what's right for me. Exactly what's right."

"Which means getting Judith to agree to following you to the ends of the earth, right?"

"Yes. Or else she stays behind."

Nochasak looked at him with an expression of shock and dismay. "You mean . . .?"

Agoak sighed and bit his lower lip. He looked gloomy as he stared at the floor.

"Yes, I know what you're thinking, Nochasak, and you're right. I love that woman. What I just said was cruel. If I didn't love her so much, do you think I'd feel so bad? I want her to understand, to share my dreams, to encourage my career. Everything you've mentioned, everything I'm capable of, my prospects here or elsewhere, I know none of that has anything to do with real Eskimo life. And it shouldn't. There comes a point where you have to leave the past behind, cut the cord. Or else become part savage again, like in the old days. Tell me, am I a traitor?"

"No. But Judith thinks so, does she?"

"Yes, that's what I was saying."

"How did she put it? In what connection?"

"I think it had something to do with my not giving help to the nomads, how it was all very well for me to have my skills and be well thought of at the bank, but what was I doing for the nomads? As it happened, there was one who went by the house that day with his wife and three children, riding a couple of sleds."

For Agoak, the really unpleasant part of the whole episode had been the moment when Judith prevented him from speaking to the Eskimo family in question, after they had all congregated in the coffee shop. He couldn't explain why, but he had taken this gesture of Judith's very badly. It had him completely baffled. He described the episode to Nochasak.

"From all you've said, it's hard to know what she's driving at. She must have something in mind, but I can't see where that leaves you.'

"From time to time, I have to recommend a nomad for a loan at the bank. There are some who are responsible, who've proved they're good risks, despite the uncertainties they have to live with. Seal hunters, Inuit who take caribou for their hides, who work trap-lines on a regular basis for the Hudson's Bay Company or fish for char on a commercial basis. As long as we know we can trust them, we never turn them away. And since I can converse with the Inuit in Inuktitut, I've managed to get a number of new customers accepted at the bank. I've also helped some of the old-timers get organized and plan their work a bit better. I think that's helping out my own kind in a way my personal abilities and development will allow. Nochasak, I'm fully aware that I'm far from. . . ."

"Have you explained what you've just told me to Judith?"

"No, not really."

"Why not?"

"I figured she wouldn't be interested."

"Are you sure?"

"At first, she was spending all her time daydreaming around the house. When I got home at night . . . you know, we were newlyweds. . . ."

"Yes, I understand."

"At dinner I'd talk a bit about what I did at the bank, but I was pretty sure she didn't have the faintest idea what my work actually involved. When she opened an account, it turned out to be the first one she'd ever had and it was a mystery to her. How could she have understood what I had to tell her about the bank?"

"You could have kept it simple. If you've been able to help out some of the nomadic Inuit, you certainly could have found the words to make her understand."

What Agoak wanted was to get Judith's undivided attention long enough to be able to describe his working day to her in his own words. For Judith had never appreciated that her husband was busy doing everything in his power to see that as many worthy, self-respecting Inuit as possible shared the fruits of his years of personal service.

Agoak didn't bother to explain all this to his friend. He felt Nochasak had understood not only the emotional aspects of their falling out, but also its more strictly ideological side, for lack of a better term. There was no need to say more.

"So what you'd like," said Nochasak, "is for me to try and explain things to Judith."

"Yes."

"On your behalf, you mean."

"Yes, since I don't feel I get through to her when I talk."

"The only problem is getting her alone. I'm at work all day and so is she."

"Can I suggest something? Let's arrange to go bowling this evening. At the last minute I'll have some piece of work to finish up at the bank and I won't join you till later, late enough so you'll have had a chance to talk to her. It's a little sneaky, but it's the only choice we have."

They agreed on the plan and Agoak got up to leave.

"I never suspected we'd reach an understanding so easily."

Agoak felt a sense of relief. He had never been quite sure that Nochasak would be willing to get involved or even that he would understand. But things were working out. The scheme for getting them together was plausible enough and Judith was unlikely to see anything suspicious in it. Which meant there might be some resolution to the problem that very evening. Was this hoping for too much?

Whatever happened in the next several hours, Agoak made up his mind to be optimistic rather than pessimistic. He breezed through his work at the bank. He didn't let his worries get in the way and in fact accomplished more than his fair share, in spite of everything. Agoak was proud of what he had done that day and as the afternoon came to a close, he realized that the excuse about having to come back in the evening was no lie. He had done so much at the counter and with the manager, who had to give final approval to some of the transactions, that he had been forced to neglect his regular duties, ones which could not be put off until the next day. He really did have to make up for lost time that evening.

CHAPTER VII

Encountering Judith back at the house at five o'clock wasn't easy for Agoak. If they had only lived in a big city, where excuses came easily and were hard to verify. . . . But Frobisher was worse than a village. Everybody knew everything. Judith would most certainly have learned already that her husband had eaten at the airport with Nochasak. It was therefore important that she have no doubts about the motives for their meeting.

"Where were you all day?" she asked her husband.

"At the airport."

"I know."

"Then why do you ask?"

"You didn't come for your break, you didn't come for lunch."

"I ate with Nochasak at the airport."

"I know that too."

"Well?"

"You might have let me know."

Agoak risked a testy remark.

"With the mood you've been in these days . . ."

Judith stood by the stove with her arms folded across her chest, looking at him.

"We've been waiting for some office furniture which is late. I went to see Nochasak so he'd telex Montreal and find out what was going on."

There was a grain of truth in what Agoak had said. It was a happy coincidence, because the girls at the bank, who were a prime source of news for Judith, would back him up. And before parting company with Nochasak, Agoak had tipped him to the story. For the moment his cover was secure.

"Since I was already out at the airport by lunchtime, I ate with Nochasak."

"Without telling me?"

"That's right."

Agoak finished his dinner. There was virtually nothing to break the silence. He sensed that Judith had her doubts and was waiting until the next day when she could check up. For the rest, she was perfectly aware she had not been in a mood designed to elicit a man's affection and concern. Was this perhaps the moment for Judith to make a clean breast of her troubles?

Though she said little and gave no promise of unburdening herself, Judith did manage a smile or two and spoke in a mild-mannered way, with the result that there was no real tension over the table. Slowly Agoak relaxed. It was perhaps to be hoped that the evening would go well and that before retiring, he and Judith would have finally found the key to a common vocabulary which had hitherto eluded them.

Suddenly Agoak was reminded of computer languages, which are so baffling to the uninitiated and yet so straightforward for those who have mastered them. It was just a matter of knowing the right passwords. He grinned at the idea. Judith noticed and looked quizzically at her husband. But Agoak was afraid to begin explaining himself, for fear of letting the cat out of the bag, so he returned to his dinner, while Judith, who had paused a moment to see if the little mystery was about to be cleared up, shrugged her shoulders and resumed eating as well.

They were watching the news afterwards, when the telephone rang. From what Judith was saying, Agoak guessed it was Nochasak's wife at the other end. After a moment Judith said, "Wait, I'll go ask him."

She turned towards Agoak and said in an unassuming tone, "Nochasak and his wife would like to go bowling with us tonight."

Agoak struck a thoughtful pose, then looked up just as Judith said, "Do you feel like it?"

Agoak nodded.

"Sure, why not?"

"That'll be fine," said Judith into the phone, "What time? Eight? We'll meet you there. Bye bye!"

They refrained from speaking while they got ready. Judith mentioned she had to iron a blouse and she set about the task briskly. At one point Agoak heard her humming while she ironed. He felt good inside. Things were definitely taking a turn for the better. There was a light at the end of the tunnel.

"Judith," he said all of a sudden.

She put down the iron and looked at her husband.

"After the day I had at the bank, I'm afraid I'm behind in my work."

"I'm not going there all alone!" she exclaimed.

"I'm not suggesting you should. You go and meet Nochasak and his wife. I'll do a few minutes' work at the bank, then join you a bit later."

"What, at ten o'clock?"

"No, I've got an hour's worth, less if anything, I promise."

"Okay."

She finished her ironing and went to the bedroom to change, while Agoak quietly rinsed and stacked the dinner dishes in preparation for the next day's washing-up, a chore he had long since taken over because of the discrepancy in their working hours.

When Judith came out of the bedroom, she was ready to leave. She nodded to indicate the dishes in the sink, looked at Agoak and muttered, "Thanks, I'd forgotten about them."

They parted company in front of the bank, Judith going on towards the bowling alley while her husband unlocked the door of his place of work. Agoak felt confident Nochasak and his wife would know how to talk to Judith. A lot could get said in an hour's time.

Agoak worked away, feeling serene and at peace with himself. By and by he was relieved to see he had finished up what he came to do. He left, locking the door behind him, as the clock struck nine.

Just as he stepped outside, Judith arrived, walking at a brisk pace.

"Come on," she said to him.

She grabbed him firmly by the arm and started pulling him in the direction of the house.

"What's going on . . .?" Agoak protested weakly.

"We'll talk about it at home," she said, keeping up her relentless pace. Agoak tried to blurt something out again further on, but Judith stopped him with a peremptory wave of the hand.

"Home I said!"

The door closed and Judith whipped off her anorak in a single motion.

"You want to talk?" she asked.

"Yes . . . This is no way to live."

"You were the one who put Nochasak up to this trick tonight!" she said harshly.

Her hands opened and closed in a convulsive movement, her features were drawn, tears welled up in her eyes.

"Hold on," said Agoak. "You're starting things off on the wrong foot already. I don't even know why you're upset."

"You don't?"

"All I can do is guess," he said quietly. "How do you expect us to reach some kind of understanding? This has been going on for weeks. We're no further ahead, our marriage is going to the dogs and we're hurting each other without even knowing why."

Judith looked down at the floor, humbled. Her voice began to break.

"Nochasak had some pretty unpleasant observations to make tonight. Maybe he's right."

"Judith, are you afraid of what might happen if we go and live in the South, in a big city?"

"Yes."

"Is there some specific reason you're afraid?"

"I'm not sure."

"You've never been to the South, Judith, and you've never known anyone to come back the worse for it."

"Yes I have."

"Who?"

"Lukasi Maniapik."

"Oh, him!"

"He lived in Montreal for three years. What was he like when he came back?"

"He was already drinking too much before he left to go there. He got into trouble down there and went to prison."

"They say he killed somebody."

"No, it was attempted murder, he didn't actually kill anybody, and apparently the judge was lenient because Lukasi was an Eskimo who wasn't used to big cities and easy access to liquor."

"There, you see?"

"Judith, think for a minute. Can you, in all honesty, compare Lukasi to a man like me?"

"I'm not saying that!"

"You're not? The way you tell it, the proof that big cities are dangerous is that Lukasi, who was a drunken bum to begin with, went to Montreal and became even more of a drunken bum. Is that apt to happen to me?"

She shook her head.

"I guess not."

"You *guess* not?"

Suddenly she burst out laughing.

"You're right, you're not like Lukasi at all."

"Let's face it: if your family, as you know them, decided to plop themselves down in Montreal or Toronto or Winnipeg, it'd be a total disaster."

"I know."

"Now be honest, do you really think that you or I would be running the same risk?"

Judith took a long breath.

"I know, I know. But there'd be other things to worry about."

"What things?" asked Agoak insistently. "What things?"

"We have everything we need here," Judith said slowly. "I used to know people who had visited here or come here to live. They all used to say that in Frobisher, an Inuk was well treated if he behaved well, that he could get work and didn't have to go without anything. People would also tell me about schools for the children, all the things there were to do, the friends there were to be made. I wasn't worried about coming here."

"But you would be about going to Montreal?"

"Yes."

"But why? Even an Eskimo, if he knows what I know, can always find work there."

"How many Eskimos are there in Montreal or any of your other cities? How many?"

"I don't know, very few. There are barely a couple of hundred Inuit in the South, in all the cities put together, if you don't count those who are just there for school or training programs."

"You see?"

"I see that as Inuit we'd be all alone, but even here we've got White friends. Down there, we'd simply have more, that's all. We speak the same language. You and I can both function in English . . ."

"With them we can."

"Yes, obviously, with them."

"But here we speak Inuktitut, our own language. In Montreal I'd have nobody to speak it with but you."

"And the children."

"You don't think for a minute that in a big city immigrants like us would ever convince their children to speak Inuktitut, do you? You know perfectly well they'd want to speak French or English."

"In Montreal, and in Toronto, I've heard lots of Italian children speaking their own language!"

"And how many Italians are there? Or Jews, or Germans? They've all got one another for support. I hear they've even got newspapers and radio and television programs in their own languages. And schools too!"

"We've got all that here," said Agoak.

"Exactly!" exclaimed Judith. "We've got it here, but we'll never have it in the South. We'd need a hundred thousand, two hundred thousand Inuit living there, whereas here we're in a position of strength. We're treated well, we have what we need. The Whites respect Inuit who work hard and live right. That's what you don't seem to understand, Agoak. We're getting somewhere in this town and I like that, it feels good. I could spend the rest of my life in Frobisher and be perfectly happy. Even if things got very expensive and I had to keep working for years, I wouldn't mind. But if we were in a big city, with all those Whites, with weather that was too hot and humid, wet snow, air pollution . . . and having to speak English day after day, without ever being able to speak Inuktitut. . . . Tell me honestly, don't you find yourself speaking English at work all day long?"

"No."

"Oh?"

"I've never really noticed. Half the customers are Inuit. The tellers are too. . . ."

"Just like the people at the movie-house, the bowling lanes, the airport. . . . The list goes on and on. It's the same for me at work: at least half the customers are Inuit or speak the language, the girls I work with are Inuit. Even the cook is an Inuk. Things would never be like that in the South, for either of us."

"So what you're saying is that you'd rather stay here. But not because you want to interfere with my career plans."

"Absolutely not, provided you limit them to what you can achieve in Frobisher, where your own kind are in the majority."

"And what if I don't limit myself?"

"What do you mean?"

"What if I was still determined to go all the way, despite everything?"

"And end up in some big city?"

"For example."

"What is it you want to know?"

"Would you come with me?"

"I know what you're thinking, Agoak. You know something about computers and you feel they've only got a limited use here."

"You're on the right track."

"Agoak, I read and watch television and keep up with what's going on in the world. I'll bet you that even if Nordair isn't making full use of computers yet. . . ."

"As far as I know," interrupted Agoak, "they already use them in the South, around Hamilton and the other places they serve."

"But not here?"

"No."

"Do you think things will be like that for long? I'm positive Nordair and other companies will soon be using computers. The government too, for that matter."

"They do say it's just a question of time," admitted Agoak.

"Well then, you could work full-time on computers, if you had a mind to. You'd be practically the only computer expert here, so there'd be almost no competition. You've got a vacation coming up next summer. There's nothing to prevent you from taking more correspondence courses, then going to Toronto during your vacation to get more practical training. No, Agoak your future is right here, among your own kind, in your own climate, where you can speak your language every evening — and even for most of the day if you want. Some day soon, you'll be able to pass along your skills to other Inuit, who may want to follow in your footsteps. You have a career to pursue here, if you want. . . ."

"You've given this a lot of thought."

"I have, yes. I might have talked about it sooner . . . I'm sure I would have in Povungnituk, if you'd trusted me, if you'd talked to me about what you were doing, what you wanted to do. But you did everything in secret, as though I couldn't appreciate what was going on. I don't talk much, Agoak, I'm aware of that. I don't say everything that's on my mind, but I keep my eyes open and I listen carefully. I retain things and I'm aware of the awful complexities of White society. While I wouldn't want to live in that society, I know we can benefit from the sort of progress the White man has brought to the Arctic. If we really want to enjoy it and get the most out of it, we should stay where we are, working hard with the skills we have."

Agoak stared at Judith in astonishment.

"I think I underestimated you," he said.

"You just didn't trust me, that's all. You thought I was an idiot because I went around without saying much and was happy just to give you love and affection."

"I must confess I really didn't know you."

"That's true, you didn't. It's just not like me to have long talks like the one we've just had. And I was getting frustrated because it looked like you were never going to understand my feelings — unless I drew you a picture, as our friends the Smiths say. I was reacting as a woman, emotionally, from the heart. I finally had to get around to telling you what I thought. And I have."

"Stay in Frobisher," mused Agoak. "Be *the* computer expert, train other Inuit. Make a career within our own little society. . . ."

"Yes!"

"Maybe that's not such a bad idea."

"It's not a bad idea at all!"

"I had the impression you wanted us to return to the nomadic life, like the ancient Inuit. . . ."

"You had that impression because I never really explained how I was thinking. Let's just say I didn't express myself very well," said Judith. "I understood what I was saying and I thought I was making myself clear. I was talking about not forgetting our origins, of being proud of them, and also about understanding the nomads."

"And helping them too!"

"Yes, especially by becoming an Inuk who's achieved something. Not just at the bank, either. It's important to serve as an example and the way to do that is to stay here, not go running off to the big city. You want to be a computer expert, fine! The only thing is, make sure those computers of yours can help *them* too, especially some of our young people, the ones who have something to offer, like you, and who could benefit by being introduced to this new world. That, to my way of thinking, is the really essential thing: you make the most of whatever advantages you've enjoyed and then pass the benefit of your experience along to other Inuit. That, as philosopher Bernard Desloges would have said, is happiness, or the next best thing anyway. It's all up to you."

Agoak, who had been listening attentively to Judith all this time, was well nestled down into his armchair, with his elbows propped up and his fingers intertwined in front of his chest. He looked pensive.

"Do you want some tea?" she asked.

Agoak nodded affirmatively and Judith went about preparing some. Agoak stared into space, lost in some reverie from which he emerged only when he began sipping the bitter, scalding beverage. He made a face, pursed his lips and sat back in his chair, with the cup balanced on the arm.

"I'm giving all this serious consideration," he said to Judith. "More than you can imagine. I'm trying to come around to your way of thinking."

Judith who had poured some tea for herself as well, was seated at an angle along one side of the table. She took a sip and savored it as she watched her husband.

"You might as well think about it at your leisure. It's not something that needs an answer. I'll see over the next few days whether you're still obsessed with the idea of leaving no matter what."

Agoak got up and marched around the living room with his hands in his pockets.

"I don't think it needs as much thinking about as all that," he said. "You were right. I created this big dream for myself, when there was no real reason to. It didn't have to take me to the four corners of North America, because it can be realized right here, after all. And we'll never be as well off anywhere else as we can be here. I have to admit it, Judith, you were right. I'm only sorry I wasn't able to see that for myself and that you had to live through some unpleasant moments."

"You had to live through some too. As far as I'm concerned, I feel sorry about not being able to make you understand my reasoning any better."

A great sense of peace — and a comforting silence — filled the house. Judith was cuddled up on Agoak's lap and he held her tenderly in his arms. Agoak felt blissfully relaxed. He smiled and Judith caressed his lips with the tip of her finger.

"What are you thinking about?" she said.

"I was thinking that in her own peculiar way, and without even knowing it, old Kuksuk was right when she yelled at me about being a traitor and having an evil spirit, an *agiortok*, in the head."

His tone became serious again, almost sombre.

"Judith, that event is something I just can't get out of my mind."

"What event?"

"When I dragged her by the arm back to her house and she was yelling insults at me. I really was betraying my own kind by wanting to emigrate to Toronto."

"Was that where you wanted to go?"

"I figured I had more of a future there than anywhere else. She was right, the poor old thing. Tomorrow I'll tell her I'm going to stay."

"You're going to stay?"

"And I'll take her a bottle of wine too."

"You're really going to stay?"

"Yes, Judith."

CHAPTER VIII

One of the things that had been aired the evening of their mutual discovery continued to haunt Agoak over the course of several days. It had come up long after their exchange of explanations, after Judith had finally spoken her mind.

For a while they just sat and exchanged caresses. As they became aroused, they set about exploring each other's bodies with their hands, unleashing a slow swell of desire which stirred their muscles. They found themselves on a straight-backed kitchen chair. They were both naked, their clothes strewn on the floor, the lights extinguished. Judith was astride Agoak's member, devouring it in long, rhythmic thrusts while he fondled her breasts, sucked her nipples and covered her neck with kisses. When Judith's hoarse moans signalled the oncoming orgasm, Agoak took hold of her hips and used his added strength to help drive his instrument of pleasure even deeper into her. They reached their climax together and Judith drenched Agoak's muscular thighs with her juices, while Agoak inundated Judith's vagina with his sperm.

They returned to the armchair, still naked but now blissfully tired, and snuggled up in the dark, where they spoke in a whisper to each other, as if they were afraid of waking up someone in the next room. This prompted Agoak to remark, "We're whispering. Nobody's asleep."

Judith giggled.

"Yes there is," she said, "and we have to be careful not to wake them."

"Who?" asked Agoak, intrigued.

"Someone," replied Judith.

Agoak pulled himself up in the chair a little and tried to catch the expression on Judith's face.

"Sweetheart, you're crazy in the head."

"No. I'm talking about the old Agoak and the old Judith, the ones from yesterday. They've gone to sleep, they've gone bye-bye. If we don't wake them up, they'll never come back. Let's try not to wake them."

Agoak threw his head back and laughed. He played with a wisp of Judith's hair.

"How would you like it if I was even more Eskimo?" he said after a while.

"You're not going to wake up the old couple are you?"

"No, I'm perfectly serious. Do you think we've lost touch with the real Inuit?"

"Perhaps a little, yes. But I want you to understand something: it's more in our attitude that we've lost touch with them. I think it's fine to be the way we are. The only thing is, there are some Inuit who haven't got as far as us and we tend to forget about them from day to day."

Agoak pushed Judith gently off his lap and made her sit on one arm of the chair.

"Am I getting that heavy already?" said Judith with a laugh. "I thought I still had a way to go."

"You know it's got nothing to do with that," said Agoak. "I've just had an idea and I'd like to discuss it."

"What's that?"

"Talking about not losing touch with the nomadic Eskimos makes me realize that I haven't done any of the things they do for a long time."

"Like what?" asked Judith a little anxiously.

"Like hunting for seal."

She laughed softly and kissed Agoak.

"Oh, is that all? I was afraid you were thinking of going on a long excursion by dog-sled!"

"Not at all," protested Agoak. "We want to get back to nature, but we don't want to overdo it. Going on a seal hunt would be enough."

"In the middle of winter?"

"Sure. It's quite easy in open water, but once the ice has set in, it's a real challenge. As long as we're going to do it at all, I'd rather give it a try in this kind of weather. I'll ask Nochasak to come along. Maybe we could go next Sunday."

"Can I come along too?" asked Judith.

"Of course!"

Agoak now had to get the expedition organized and that gave him cause for concern. Nothing seemed to work out quite as Agoak imagined it would. The first thing he realized was that Inuk or not, he wasn't actually equipped to go and hunt anything at all. The situation was much the same for Nochasak, who had given his only remaining rifle to his elder son two years previously. Between them they had no guns, no ammunition, not even a hunting knife. A visit to the store was in order and this Nochasak and Agoak did one day on their lunch-hour. When they came out, they were well equipped and ready for anything. Agoak bought both a rifle and a shotgun for himself, then another rifle and shotgun, as well as three 100-round boxes of ammunition for each weapon and three hunting knives of different sizes, with leather sheathes.

Nochasak was flabbergasted.

"You've got a whole arsenal there," he commented.

"Judith expressed interest in coming along with us. How about your wife?"

"I doubt it. She leads a sedentary life here in Frobisher and hasn't been on a hunting expedition since the children were small, a good twenty years ago. Even the times I've gone she hasn't wanted to come along. She used to go out a lot as a girl with her father and her brothers, but as she says herself, that's all behind her now."

"Judith used to hunt when she was younger too. But that was with the men in her family, who are all drunkards. It couldn't have been very pleasant."

Judith was happy. The arms Agoak had purchased were among the best, and she handled them with obvious relish. She apparently knew quality when she saw it.

"I used to be afraid of guns and afraid of hunting when I lived at home," she said. "I never knew when one of my drunken relatives might start firing a gun at random. Whenever they were cleaning their guns in the house, I'd start to shake all over and I'd hide somewhere as far away as possible. I'd often go hide in the mission, for example, just to be far away. And whenever they forced me to go on a hunt with them, I'd be terrified from start to finish."

She stroked the long, smooth barrels and smiled.

"It'll be completely different with you, Agoak. I'll go as often as you like."

"Do you know how to handle a gun?"

Judith worked the bolt of her rifle in a convincing manner.

"Certainly," she replied. "I just might be the one who gets the seal on Sunday!"

That evening Agoak pondered what Judith had said. Maybe she

was right; maybe she was more likely to make a kill than he was. Apart from anything else, he had stopped hunting while still very young. As his father had not hunted and he didn't have any brothers or sisters his own age, his hunting had been confined almost exclusively to childhood expeditions with young friends. He had done so little hunting, so long ago, that he barely remembered the essentials. He probably still remembered how to shoot, because that's a skill you don't lose. But could he actually hunt?

At one point he asked Nochasak, "Do you remember what's involved in hunting seal?"

"Oh yes. I go on seal hunts every year, both winter and spring."

Hearing Judith say she was likely to be the one to make the first kill didn't really surprise Agoak, even if it left him feeling a little unsettled. He kept coming back to the idea that Judith wanted more than anything for him to be an Inuk. Unfortunately, he had long ago forgotten the most basic rituals of the traditional way of life. He had become estranged from both the primitive outlook and the daily activities with which it was associated. Coming as he did from a family who had chosen to earn their living from something as sendentary as stone carving, living his life divorced from the ancient Eskimo traditions, which he knew only second-hand, by word of mouth, Agoak now realized that while he had come a long way in a short time, retracing his steps would be a good deal more difficult. And what would Judith think if the expedition turned out to be something of a failure? That would certainly make Agoak look bad. How would that make Judith feel?

Of course, they had had a searching discussion about the future of their relationship, about their future together. Judith's own attachment to the traditional Eskimo costume was unequivocal. What did she have in mind for Agoak. That he had come to look like a White or like an Inuk? Perhaps the hunt would bring them face to face with some stark realities. Agoak had his pride to think of, first as a man, then as an Inuk, and the prospect of being humiliated filled him with anxiety. . . . The hunt had been his idea and it would be difficult to back out now. As he went to bed that evening, he wondered if it had been such a good idea after all. He had a fitful sleep.

Sunday arrived and the morning seemed favorable.

"I've probably heard hundreds of seal-hunt stories being recounted," Agoak said to his friend as they stood outside packing their gear. "I guess I never paid attention. In any case, I never absorbed much. So once the three of us get out there, don't be surprised if I'm a little hesitant. I don't really know anything about it."

Nochasak explained a few things.

"In the spring, you can hunt seal in the open water or, anywhere there are islands, on beaches or rock outcroppings by the shore. In winter it's different. The seal is under the ice, where he's hollowed out an *agloo* for himself, a kind of chamber with an air-hole. That's where he comes to breathe. If the weather's very cold, you can see the mist of his breath and even his black snout as it pokes up through the ice. Or you can go looking for the hole, but that takes much longer. Once you've found it, you enlarge it enough to give you easy access to the chamber underneath. You wait a little while somewhere close by, keeping absolutely still, and sometimes the seal will haul out and stay on the ice for a few moments. If you're a good shot, you stay where you are, wait for the mist and fire at his snout. If you think you've hit him, you enlarge the hole and with a little luck he'll be there, dead, floating in the chamber. But it's not always that simple. Sometimes he doesn't die so quickly. I can remember times when I've had to poke around under the ice to find him. It's definitely much easier in the spring."

Agoak nodded in agreement.

"The best thing to do is follow you and Judith and just see how it goes."

"Of course."

"The important thing for me, if I'm going to take a shot, is that I don't miss."

"What does Judith have to say about it all?"

"She says she's going to make the first kill!"

"Fine, let her have her opinion, see she gets her chance."

But Agoak was not sure things would be so simple. They left the house by snowmobile and headed for the wide-open expanse of the bay, which still had only a sprinkling of snow on it. Agoak had a queasy feeling in the pit of his stomach.

He realized that proposing this hunting expedition had been more or less an act of bravado on his part and that he was about to reap the rather chancy consequences. It perhaps would have been better to prove himself by undertaking feats about which he felt more confident, which the Eskimo that refused to die in Judith might still find convincing . . . but it was too late for second thoughts.

"It can't be helped," Agoak mused as he rode along with his wife in the sled behind Nochasak's snowmobile. "I played the wrong hand, but I've played it. If I lose out, I'll have nobody to blame but myself."

It took them a good hour to reach the spot Nochasak thought would serve them best in their endeavor. They had left at dawn, or what passes for dawn in the Arctic, where night and day are difficult to distinguish, and they were scarcely aware of the passing of time. All around them was a bluish half-light, while the long reddish-gold line of the midnight sun stretched along the flat, endless horizon.

Nochasak stopped the machine, slowly climbed out, looked carefully in every direction, took a few steps and crouched down to scan the surface of the ice as far as the eye could see.

Judith then stirred, got out of the sled and went and crouched at an angle to Nochasak. She too kept as still as possible and looked carefully out over the vast whiteness.

Not wanting to be left behind, Agoak followed suit. He recalled the technique of looking for the breath which Nochasak had mentioned and he was anxious to find out if he could spot a seal for himself that way.

The three dark masses in their furry anoraks remained as motionless as statues for a long time. Agoak reminded himself that keeping still was essential. Any animal living on such flat, deserted wastes was sensitive to, and shy of, the slightest movement. Before the seal came too far out of its air-hole, it would scrutinize the landscape and dive to the depths at the slightest suspicion of anything unusual. It would then be some time until it reappeared. Agoak, like his two companions, was therefore most careful not to budge while he examined every inch of the icy plain.

Although in his heart of hearts he felt cut off from what he termed the "real" Inuit, Agoak was in fact the first to whistle a quiet signal to the others that he had spotted something. Some distance away, in the blue air just above the ice, two puffs of mist had appeared, lit from behind by the morning sun, which hung low over the horizon. Agoak did not move right away, but waited till they appeared again. Several minutes passed before the seal came back to the surface. This time, perhaps because he was paying more attention, the puff of vapor seemed higher, clearer and sharper. Using instincts he never imagined he still possessed, he trained his eyes carefully on certain barely discernable features of the terrain and committed them to memory. First he noticed there was a slight depression in the ice and a little beyond that, a rounded, but clearly defined hump lying directly to the right of the spot where the first two puffs had appeared.

With the third puff, which he had no trouble getting a fix on in the surrounding landscape, Agoak alerted his companions. Nochasak immediately crawled over to the spot where Agoak was crouched down.

"Did you see something?" he whispered.

He too was following instincts he thought he had long since lost. He spoke as quietly as possible, knowing how acute the seal's hearing was and how easily sound travelled through ice which had little snow cover. But he had enough to go on now that the mist had been spotted. It remained to get close to the animal's agloo, so that they could put the rest of their strategy into action.

Nochasak then said to Agoak and Judith, who had also joined them, "We're going to walk very carefully, almost on tip-toes, over to the agloo."

"Should we be ready to fire?" asked Judith.

"The ice isn't too thick," replied Nochasak, "so I think we'd be better off enlarging the hole. I think the seal will haul out on to the ice."

"How do you know?" asked Agoak in a curious tone.

"It's not a matter of knowing," said Nochasak. "Apparently, it's quite unpredictable. The Inuit I've hunted with, including some of the real old-timers, have told me it's not something you can really predict."

"I guess we'll just have to wait and see," said Agoak. "I've had hunters tell me the same thing."

"I remember from when I was young and used to go out hunting," commented Judith in turn, "that both methods were used. However, a hole in the ice meant we should wait. It was safer. But you still have to be very careful not to miss the seal, otherwise he'll be back in the water in two seconds and you won't see him again for a long time."

"We can do it either way," said Nochasak. "Get closer or shoot at the mist from here."

"It takes a good shot to make a kill that way," said Agoak.

"An expert," said Judith. "There was someone like that in Povungnituk who never missed, apparently."

"It certainly wasn't me," said Agoak.

"No, it wasn't, Agoak," said Judith giggling.

"And I'm way out of practice," added Nochasak. "How about you, Judith?"

She threw up her hands.

"You expect me to take a chance on spoiling everything?"

"Okay," said Nochasak, "we'll go and dig out the hole. Follow me — and don't make any noise."

They moved back to the sled, guided by Nochasak, and pulled out their axes. Then Agoak took the lead and, with their eyes riveted to the irregularities in the ice which acted as their reference points, they walked along as quietly as possible. Agoak raised his arm once, in midstride, to point to the puffs of mist, which seemed to drift higher and higher as they got closer and closer.

They all stopped for a moment when they realized how near they were to their goal. From that location it was possible to make out the hole itself: it was darker than the surrounding ice and stood out quite distinctly in the faint light. The seal had dived back into the water, so they began moving forward again, more cautiously than ever. Nochasak whispered, "It's getting tricky now. We can't be too close to the agloo when he comes up to breathe, otherwise he'll notice us here and might disappear for good."

Timing themselves on the basis of the seal's breathing cycle, they stopped in their tracks a little farther on, and just then the mist reappeared. It took them several minutes, inching carefully forward, before they reached the vicinity of the agloo. There they stopped again, crouched down and waited. They despaired of ever seeing the seal again. Then, all of a sudden, they spotted the creature's snout poking up through the ice, heard him draw a long, hoarse breath and watched the warm mist rise into the air. The next moment he was gone. Nochasak was on his feet in a flash, ax in hand, chopping furiously. Responding with similar alacrity, Judith and Agoak rushed to Nochasak's side, where they too began working feverishly at their millenial task, as though it were second nature to them.

As they chopped away, Nochasak said, "He's gone down a long way, to feed. When he comes back, we'll have to be in position."

Then, more by intuition than experience, Nochasak grunted a warning to the other two.

"Watch it, he's on his way!"

They moved back a few feet and waited in a crouch. The hole was bigger now and the seal hesitated momentarily. He swam back and forth, looking around as he did, but saw and heard nothing. Feeling emboldened, he thrust his muzzle a little farther out of the water, exhaled noisily and then, with a long whistling sound, inhaled the brisk fresh air.

As soon as he had dived to the depths again, the three Inuit returned to their task. This time when Nochasak sounded the alert, there was an opening in the ice measuring at least one square metre. The weather was not yet cold enough for the green, sluggish waters of Frobisher Bay to freeze over very quickly. They waited again for the seal to return and familiarize himself with the sudden changes in his environment. He disappeared once more, and the three hunters all loaded their rifles and moved back rapidly about twenty metres, where they crouched down motionless, their weapons at the ready.

There was nothing more they could do. Either the seal would keep coming up simply to breathe and then dive again, or else he would haul out onto the ice to give his exhausted muscles a rest from continuous swimming. It all depended on what the beast had been up to during the preceding hours. And that, of course, was something nobody knew but the seal himself. All the three hunters could do, therefore, was wait.

Trusting entirely to their instincts now, the three Inuit sat on the ground with their weapons in place, aiming at the newly enlarged hole in the vastness of the ice. The stamina which they were able to call upon was strictly atavistic; no White could ever tolerate the strain on the constitution which built up over such long periods of time. Even Agoak, the least seasoned of them all and the one most sheltered from such trials, held his position without moving a muscle. He was curious himself to see how long he could last and was surprised to discover that he did not feel weakened by the ordeal.

The time wore on. The seal kept coming up for air at regular intervals and showed no real signs of concern, nor much curiosity either. The silence and the stillness reassured him. He kept breathing his fill, then disappearing again. At one point Nochasak sighed in an uncharacteristic way, but neither Judith nor Agoak paid any attention. They maintained their vigil, hardly venturing to blink their eyes.

Suddenly, Agoak was overcome by a strange sense of foreboding and the next moment, to his great surprise, the seal appeared and began to roll up onto the ice. Half-way out of the water he paused and clung to the edge of the ice, while he took a long, careful look at his surroundings. Nothing stirred; there were no signs of life. Feeling reassured, the seal pulled himself out of the water and onto the ice in a series of slow, flowing movements, then, breathing a long sigh of relief, stretched out on the ice, where he made himself a kind of nest in the thin layer of snow.

The shots rang out, a split-second apart: the seal was thrown into the air, then fell back dead. It was quite apparent that the first shot had been fired by Judith and that, from the motion of the seal's body, she had hit it right in the head. The glory was incontestably hers.

Judith stood up, smiling timidly and gesturing in a manner that indicated disbelief. And in an equally disbelieving tone of voice, she repeated over and over again, "I killed him! I killed him!"

Then, turning to her husband and to Nochasak, she said, "Excuse me."

Agoak just laughed.

"You should see yourself right now," he said. "You look like a little girl who's just been caught in the act."

Judith couldn't help laughing either.

"What a surprise!" she said. "I was sure one of you would get him first."

They went over to have a look at their prey. Judith's bullet had indeed struck the head, right in the middle. They noticed two other wounds, one in the neck and the other right down near the tail.

Pointing to this last wound, Agoak made a face and said, "That must be mine." He then added, to the great amusement of the others, "It's a good thing for me I'm an accountant and not a nomad who has to hunt to stay alive. Mind you," he said, pointing to his wife, "if I was, I'd have Judith with me and I could manage."

Agoak could not have put it better.

Nochasak went off to get the snowmobile and drove it back to the spot where the seal's remains lay. He got out his knife and pointed to the carcass.

"I can flense it right here," he said. "We'll take what we want and throw the rest back in the water so the wolves won't come for it."

But Judith seemed to have another idea in mind.

"There's something I'd like to do," she said, smiling at Agoak. "It would be just like the old days."

"What were you thinking of?" asked Agoak.

"I'd like to take the seal back to the house and cut it up there."

"You want to do it yourself?" asked Agoak.

"Yes. I used to do it all the time in Povungnituk."

"And you want to do it in the house?"

"Yes."

"Where?"

"On the kitchen floor."

"Right on the kitchen floor?"

"I can clean it up afterwards. Will you let me, Agoak?"

The two Inuit looked at each other. They both shrugged their shoulders.

"If you'd really like to, Judith."

"I would," said Judith. "That way we'll be sure to get the best pieces, and we can share the booty with Nochasak. Do you enjoy having seal at home?" she asked the Inuk.

"We don't eat it very often, but when we do we really enjoy it."

"You'll have more than your fill this time!"

They set about getting the animal moved. It was a good-sized male, weighing about 100 kilos. After the two men had heaved it onto the sled, the little group headed in the direction of town, the lights from which gave a reddish tinge to the sky.

Back at the house, Agoak, who had been mulling things over during the return journey, seemed less enthusiastic. Judith was dismayed to see him pulling a long face as they carted the seal into the kitchen.

"Something's come over you," said Judith. "Look at yourself...."

Agoak was pouting.

"What's the matter?" asked Judith.

"Do you realize what butchering it in the house will involve?"

"Yes."

"Do we have to be true to our roots by splattering blood and guts all over the place?"

Nochasak seemed to be amused by Agoak's question. Judith burst out laughing.

"For God's sake, Agoak, let's just do it. You're like a dog who's afraid of his own shadow."

"No, really, do you have any idea what kind of a mess a butchered seal is going to make in here?"

The White man's outlook had apparently so affected Agoak's thinking that Judith and Nochasak felt cause for concern over his reaction. Powerless to overcome his aversion, Agoak was also aware that he was upsetting Judith. She had made her request. Did this mean she was really anxious for a wholesale return to the traditional life? Or had he misunderstood?

It was the moment of truth. Agoak stared in grim silence at the carcass lying on the ground and felt incapable of either going on or turning back. Coming to terms with his aversion, on the one hand, and exercising his authority in order to stop Judith, on the other, were equally untenable alternatives. The ink was hardly dry on the peace treaty they had signed only a few days before, and it would not do to run roughshod over it already. But Agoak couldn't remain ambivalent forever. A decision had to be made and Agoak's decision was to wash his hands of the problem, in effect, to break his word. He said brusquely, "You can do whatever suits you. I'm going out." As he reached the door he turned around and added, "You can interpret this any way you like."

Thanks to Agoak's gesture, they were right back to square one again. Even after he was long gone, Judith was still standing by the seal with an expression of astonishment on her face. She seemed saddened, but not angered, by what had happened. She lifted her head and looked at Nochasak.

"I think I went too far," she said.

He shook his head pensively.

"Too far, too fast," he said. "You weren't brought up in the same way as him. As he points out, his family led a sit-down life and earned their living like Whites. He left home quite young to go to school. He probably never saw a seal being butchered, whereas it's nothing unusual for you. . . . Yes, I think you did go too far."

"I guess I shouldn't have," she muttered.

"On the other hand," continued Nochasak, "did you see how Agoak behaved today? He was like a real, honest-to-goodness Inuk out there. It was Agoak who saw the seal's breath first."

Judith wrung her hands and between clenched teeth said, "I actually saw it before him — but I didn't want to say anything."

There was a pause, then Nochasak said, "So did I."

Judith sighed, walked around the carcass of the seal and stopped at Nochasak's side, touching his arm.

"I think the best thing would be for you to take the seal with you. If you've still got any meat a little while from now, you can give me some to put in the freezer. For the time being, however, I'd better just forget about it."

Then, in a tone of humility, she added, "We did the wrong thing just now."

"So we did," Nochasak added in agreement.

Thus, while originally designed to placate Judith, the seal hunt had managed to ruin what might otherwise have been a most enjoyable Sunday.

In a contrary frame of mind and with his pace accelerated by pent-up anger, Agoak had quickly covered the distance to the hotel and now sat in the bar slowly sipping a beer. He drew up a mental balance-sheet for the day and found positive feelings on the credit side. On the debit side, however, was this notion of Judith's about butchering the seal at home, which she seemed to think would be barely more complicated than slicing up a loaf of bread for dinner. It was obviously not quite as simple as that; what was not so obvious, on the other hand, was the strange compulsion that lay behind her actions. Was it inherited? Agoak could not rule out the possibility. But was it also necessary for him, for Agoak, to be influenced in his every word and deed by the past? He was in a position to help his fellow Inuit, to lend them support, to promote their success. He could be a hero to them in today's terms; a man revered and respected. He didn't mind the idea of being a social catalyst; but he saw no necessity for any return to the past. Agoak had ancestors who had eaten human flesh. Did this mean Judith was liable to suggest they devour someone on a future Sunday outing, in deference to tradition?

The idea was ridiculous and Agoak knew full well that nothing of the sort was about to happen. Still, such a far-fetched notion seemed to him the logical extension of Judith's line of reasoning.

The bar was exasperatingly noisy, smokey and jammed with people. Agoak stayed put because he knew how to withdraw and become deaf and blind to what was around him. Besides, it would be no better elsewhere. The coffee shop was also packed. It was just as well to stay here, absorbed in his own thoughts, so he could sort things out.

What he could not get over was being asked to embrace two mutually incompatible ways of life. For him it was enough to live in harmony with those around him. Such harmony engendered mutual respect, and made race unimportant. Accomplishing the goals one had set for oneself seemed to him to be enough. On the other hand, he had no quarrel with the way his ancestors had lived. There had been good reason for it. They did not wander the length and breadth of the Arctic out of some misplaced desire for freedom, but rather in the interests of sheer survival. Agoak had nothing to reproach them for. Yet certain behavioral patterns, even if common to an entire people, could always change. It was no longer necessary for any Inuk to pursue his survival over vast distances. Nowadays it was possible for him to stay put and survive, once he realized what opportunities lay close at hand.

So it was for Agoak, who certainly had no objections to blazing a trail for as many Inuit as needed his help. But in order to accomplish this on their behalf, was it absolutely necessary for him to adopt their way of life down to the last detail? They had all lived — and as it happened some of them still lived — off the wildlife that roamed that part of the world. They had done this for so long that they were perhaps no longer capable of changing course and could only barge blindly ahead, indifferent to the opportunities being offered them for a new and comparatively comfortable existence.

Agoak thought back to the evening in Toronto which he had spent at an English folk festival. Everything about it, the costumes, the food, the songs, the dancing, drew on Anglo-Saxon tradition. But the next day, as Agoak was quick to notice, the past was put aside for the sake of the present, something he found quite understandable. Furthermore, the sense of nostalgia evoked had a restrained quality about it and stopped short of any excessively romanticized view of the past. He was finally able to put his finger on what bothered him about Judith's attitude: she had a yearning for the past, but was incapable of distinguishing beneficial traditions from those that were simply irrelevant or unpalatable.

There was nothing Agoak could do about the fact that gutting, skinning and butchering a seal made him sick, and always had. He had agreed to Judith's request in a moment of weakness, while they were still outdoors, stimulated by the bracing fresh air and wide open spaces. But once back in the warmth of the house, he recalled the foul smell and gelatinous consistency of seal guts laid bare by the knife. He had only ever had to witness such a scene twice as a boy and both times he had thrown up violently. Everything in him rebelled at the very thought.

How could he explain to his wife that, as an Inuk born and bred, he had so little enthusiasm for the ancient customs? What did being a man signify for Judith? Agoak was still mystified about her feelings and had no desire to be enlightened on the subject just at the moment.

Ensconced in the bar of the hotel, Agoak continued to mull over the events of the previous several hours, and even took stock of his life as a whole. Yet one thought began pressing in on him with greater and greater urgency: he had to return home. He waved his hand, asked for the bill, paid and left.

His watch read six o'clock. Had there been enough time? Agoak might walk in the door and find that the butchering was still not finished. However, a vague childhood memory told him less time was needed than had elapsed that afternoon. As he walked out of the building, he could see his house in Ikaluit, although from this distance he could not make out anything through the windows.

He was back in the twinkling of an eye. As he got closer he noticed that Nochasak's snowmobile was gone. That was a good sign. He quickened his pace and strode through the door. Judith, who had been watching television, got up to greet her husband. The kitchen, including the double sink, was clean, and everything seemed to be in place. Agoak gave Judith a puzzled look.

"I didn't flense the seal after all," she said slowly. "I gave it to Nochasak. He'll be bringing a little meat for us to put in the freezer."

Agoak was astonished, but despite a burning curiosity, he said nothing.

"Agoak," said Judith, "I'm sorry."

"Sorry for what?"

"For what I did. I was cruel and insensitive. It's not a thing somebody who loves you should have done."

"You're crazy!"

"Yes, I know. I was and I still am. It's all my fault. I said all the wrong things. Can you forgive me?"

"I thought it was really important for you to flense the seal yourself."

"No! I said that . . . I don't know why I said it. Maybe because I thought it would be fun. It brought back nice memories."

"You see?"

"Not necessarily nice memories, I wouldn't want to relive any of that. I think when I first flensed a seal, I had a kind of need to tear flesh. It was subconscious revenge against my family for the life I had to lead."

"Judith, try to forget."

"Yes, I know I should try to. But when I saw the carcass on the ice, it brought so many things flooding back that I couldn't think straight anymore. I didn't even bother to ask you how you felt about the whole thing. It never occurred to me that you might look at it differently. When Nochasak reminded me after you left that you grew up with a family who worked indoors and never went hunting, I realized what I'd done, but by then it was too late. So I gave the carcass to Nochasak. All of a sudden, I didn't want it anymore."

"What have you been doing all this time?" asked Agoak.

"I just sat down. I thought you'd be at the hotel, but since you hardly drink at all, I wasn't worried."

"You could've come to get me."

"I didn't want to be with other people. I had to do some thinking, because I realized once again I hadn't said everything I should have said, or maybe I just didn't say it the right way. Agoak, I'm an Eskimo woman and I'm proud of the fact that we come from an ancient culture and that our people managed to survive very well under extremely bad conditions. And I know they'll meet other challenges if they have to. But in spite of what I'm saying, I'm also very proud of having received an education from the Whites. I'm determined to remain an Inuk, but not to the point where it spoils our life. I'm going to behave in a perfectly rational way, Agoak, just like you, because that's the only way we can live right now."

She smiled and wrapped her arms around him.

"And that's the last time I'll ever suggest we gut and butcher a seal on the kitchen floor, I promise."

Despite their reconciliation, and the sense of physical release attained before they switched off the lights, Agoak and Judith slept badly, though this had nothing to do with the nervous tension built up over the day. They had had nothing more to say to each other for the moment and were well disposed to enjoying a good night's sleep. The problem was the ruckus created by Tomasic Papik's dogs.

In the middle of winter, Frobisher is not a particularly peaceful place, day or evening, least of all on a Sunday. During the week, the splutter of snowmobile engines, along with the occasional Bombardier carrying freight or passengers, forms an ever-present backdrop of sound. By evening the heavy-duty vehicles are back in the garage, but the snowmobiles can still be heard, since both Whites and Inuit use them for transport, or simply for recreational purposes. For some years now dogs have been getting rarer and rarer, and only the real nomads are still likely to arrive in town with a pack of Huskies. Ikaluit had not seen a single dog until that Sunday, when Tomasic Papik, Agoak's neighbor three doors away, turned up around noon, for no apparent reasons, with two magnificent teams of Huskies, who were as pure in their breeding as they were boisterous, irascible, noisy and quarrelsome.

Though most of Frobisher was finally asleep, the air was filled with the cacophonous, age-old sound of dogs yelping and howling, a sound utterly characteristic of the Arctic, even if it is one now largely replaced by the high-pitched drone of the snowmobile.

CHAPTER IX

The days went by and life returned to normal. If the engine had been misfiring for a while, it was now back in tune and running as it should. Agoak and Judith took up where they had left off, without regret or remorse.

And then, one fateful afternoon, while Agoak chatted with a customer at the bank and Judith busied herself serving a group of Inuit at a table in the coffee shop, an aircraft loomed over Resolution Island and the Strait of Gabriel and made contact with the control tower in Frobisher.

"Request pattern, request pattern."

The plane identified itself. It was a Lear jet of Canadian registry. From where the Lear was just at that moment, it would have taken a Beaver, Otter or DC-3 some time to reach its destination, but this was a jet-propelled aircraft and it flew at speed. No sooner had it asked for flight path information than it was radioing:

"Request permission to land. Give instrument reading and strip number."

Again the pilot gave his call letters.

A few minutes later, the sleek, elegant craft touched down on the runway. Two men climbed out and immediately began inquiring, "Is there anywhere to eat? Come on, come on!"

They were hungry and wanted some action out of the ground crew. They also needed directions and it was in fact Nochasak, who happened to be crossing the tarmac at that particular moment, who explained to them where to find the Bombardier which would take them to the coffee shop. At that time of day, with the hotel dining room not yet open, it was the most presentable spot to have a bite to eat.

91

And so it was that on this particular day two men walked into the nearly deserted coffee shop, where it became Judith's responsibility to serve them. Fate works in strange ways, for while Emilie Outsanuk was working the same shift as Judith, she was not the one who happened to take these particular orders. How easily it could have been otherwise.

The men were White, but of a sort Judith had rarely seen before. What struck her about them right away was the quality of their clothes. They were brand new, and Judith had never seen fabric so fine or so beautifully cut. Their watches, their rings, the cigarette case and the lighter which lay on the table, all attested to the fact they were rich and very sure of themselves, even arrogant. They stared incessantly at Judith, examining her up and down, taking in every detail. She felt them undressing her with their eyes. She had pretty breasts and, under normal circumstances, she was proud of the fact. But standing by their table she felt as though she were stark naked and the piercing stares were actually fondling her breasts. She shuddered and went stiff with resentment. A strange sense of revulsion swept through her. The two men in question were young and handsome as gods as well. But there was something written on their faces, something Judith couldn't quite understand and didn't want to understand. She was pleasant all the same. She had to be. The manager was nearby and keeping a close watch on the two strangers and no doubt on Judith as well.

What really unsettled her was being confronted once again by an attitude she had known as a child, when Whites of this kind would come through Povungnituk and act in an insulting manner, addressing the Inuit in a tone at once condescending and threatening. This kind of arrogance, though rare in the Arctic today, was something Judith could never tolerate, especially now that she was part of Frobisher society and expected to be treated accordingly.

Somehow the two men were almost polite with her, even if they seemed rather too fascinated by her body, her hair, her smile . . . and even said so! At the same time, they insisted on talking to her as though she were a child.

"How old are you?"

She suppressed her resentment and smiled, as she felt obliged to do going so far in fact as to look a little flirtatious, since the customer is after all, always right.

"Old enough to be married," she replied. "What can I get you?"

The one who looked to be the older of the two made a face, closed his eyes and asked, "Do you know what a club sandwich is?"

He asked the question in a contemptuous tone, as though expecting an answer in the negative.

"Of course I do," said Judith dryly.

This seemed to disappoint them and the younger one gave a facetious smile.

"So bring two club sandwiches."

"We have three kinds," said Judith. She handed them the menus she'd been holding. "Would you like to choose one?" She turned on her heel and said as she left, "I'll be right back."

She walked over towards the cash, where Emilie Outsanuk was standing idle for the moment. The manager came over and looked at Judith.

"Everything okay?" he asked, more by way of a warning than anything else.

"I don't know who those two are," said Judith in a rage, "but I could just kill them!"

"Shhh . . .," said the manager.

Emilie put her fingertips on Judith's arm.

"Do you want me to take over?"

"No," said Judith brusquely, "I can manage."

She returned to the table and stood tapping her heel.

"Are you ready to order?"

"What time does the hotel dining room open?" asked one of the men.

"Six o'clock," said Judith.

"We'll wait. Bring us some coffee."

Judith went to get the two coffees, brought them to the table and returned to the cash desk, turning her back to the two strangers. Other customers drifted in and were served by Emilie, while Judith sat alone with her elbows on the counter, fully aware that the two men were still staring at her.

Emilie stopped in midstream to say to Judith, "They just won't give up, and now they're whispering to each other while they look you over."

Judith shrugged her shoulders.

"I'm off in ten minutes, then they're all yours."

She tried to get the men out of her mind and instead planned what she would do after she finished her shift and returned home. That Saturday they had done a huge shopping at the meat and grocery department of the Bay. After checking the cupboards, the refrigerator and the freezer, Judith had decided their supplies were altogether too low and so with Agoak's approval, they had purchased roast upon roast — beef, pork, even lamb — an enormous turkey, several good-sized capons and a large quantity of canned goods, which included several more meat items among them. As Judith had said with a giggle to Agoak, "I got up feeling like some meat this morning and look what it's done for us. We're going to go broke at these prices!"

"Still," said Agoak, "we had hardly anything left in reserve."

As she got ready to go home, it occurred to Judith that a hefty steak would make a delicious dinner. Unfortunately, what she had purchased was already in the freezer and couldn't be used that quickly. For just such a contingency — leaving aside the canned goods — there was some bacon in the refrigerator, though that would hardly make a real feast. She made a mental note to be better organized next day and take out something to thaw in time for dinner, then resigned herself to fixing bacon and eggs for Agoak that evening. If prepared with the appropriate amount of love, that would do for this once.

After her moment of frustration had passed and she had recovered her good humor, she set off for Ikaluit, striding along vigorously, humming and whistling, feeling enormously content and somehow rejuvenated.

She strode into the house at the same brisk pace, in the same mood of elation, closed the door behind her and set about tidying up a bit and doing a few of the usual daily chores. At five o'clock she started the dinner, so that by the time Agoak got back home, the bacon would be cooked and the eggs would be ready for the frying pan. With some toast, slices of cheddar and a few pickles, it would be a simple but restorative meal. Judith performed her tasks with a sense of joy.

After Judith had gone and their coffees were paid for, the two visitors left the coffee shop in an unhurried manner. They stepped outside and glanced around at their environment in the sombre light of the midnight sun. But what they were concentrating their attention on was Judith as she walked down the hill towards Ikaluit. One of them, the younger of the two, laughed sarcastically.

"Shall we?" he said.

The other man looked undecided. He hesitated.

"What's the matter, Bob?" asked the younger man.

His companion shook his head doubtfully as he examined their surroundings, the big building behind them, the layout of the rest of the town. The other man was straining at the leash.

"She's only a native!" he exclaimed, in the sort of tone characteristic of an American talking about Blacks. They finally made up their minds and started walking slowly in the direction of the house which they had just seen Judith enter. They made their way cautiously through the snow, something they were obviously unaccustomed to doing. Nor were their expensive boots of much help either.

"What do you want from her?" asked the older man.

"Oh you know, talk to her, kiss her a little, see if she's as built as she looks. I've never had a chance to see an Eskimo's tits before and I don't want to miss the opportunity.

"And what if she makes a fuss?" he asked, pointing to the town all around. "It's no village."

"What're you worried about? Do you think anybody here listens to the natives?" he said, again stressing the word "natives" in a tone of profound contempt. He gave a cavalier wave of the hand.

"I'll throw a few American tens on the floor and you just watch how fast she gets down on her hands and knees to pick them up. After that I guarantee you she'll head for the bedroom with us and show us a real good time for our trouble. Did you see those eyes? Wave a few bucks in front of them and watch them light up."

"What if there's somebody else in the house?"

"We'll check that out. We can always make up some story. . . ."

They had arrived in front of the house and through the window they could see Judith moving around. They could also see the table was set.

"She's alone," said the younger man.

The one called Bob whispered, "You're right, she really is good-looking."

"You see? You're horny for her too."

"I wouldn't kick her out of bed, that's for sure. Anyway, we're practically at the North Pole, thousands of miles from home, so we deserve a little fun."

"I think we're going to have a ball tonight."

Judith had just begun removing the first few strips of bacon from the package when the door suddenly burst open. Someone had barged in without even knocking.

Judith was astonished to see the two customers from the coffee shop standing there. They looked tall and imposing in the low-ceilinged house. Their voices were loud and harsh and they snickered sarcastically. Thunderstruck and momentarily at a loss for words, Judith stared at the intruders, then managed to blurt out, "What are you doing here? What do you want?"

The men just kept laughing and moving towards her, drowning out the poor girl's protests with their brutal comments.

"What do you want?!" she said again, almost screaming.

"I think maybe we want to use the phone," replied one of the men in a tone of mock deference.

"There isn't any telephone here! Get out of here!"

By this time, however, the younger man had already grabbed her. He held her by the waist with one arm as he tried to take hold of a breast with the other hand. Judith struggled as best she could, but before long both men were wrestling with her and tearing off her clothes. Judith managed to grab the pan in which the bacon had started to fry and threw the boiling fat in the younger man's face. He howled with rage and punched Judith right in the face as hard as he could. With her lip split open, her nose bleeding and her cheek bruised, Judith fell back, stunned by the blow. In a sudden burst of fury, the two men tore off the rest of her clothes, then the older man threw her on the floor and held her down while his companion pulled out his penis and drove it into the girl. He pounded away at her with his lower body, determined to achieve immediate gratification. Judith screamed and writhed as she attempted to dislodge the huge glistening organ, but her assailants were too strong and kept her pinned to the floor.

Just then, Agoak came in, unnoticed. Still wearing his parka and mukluks, he ran straight into the bedroom, in a blind, terrible rage. He grabbed a rifle and a hunting knife and bounded into the kitchen. He fired a shot and wounded the younger man, who had been raping Judith. The two men leapt to their feet, but a second shot struck the older man. Then with his knife held high over his head, Agoak sprang on the two wounded men like a crazed panther. He stabbed and slashed in broad strokes, hacking off strips of clothing and skin and flesh. Nothing could stop him, neither the assailants' pleas for mercy nor their feeble attempts at defending themselves. Agoak continued at his butchery until the two men finally collapsed, half-naked, with blood pouring from a dozen wounds, their costly outfits cut to ribbons. As they moaned in agony, they tried their best to push away this madman who was bent on killing them.

"Stop, stop," pleaded one of them. "We'll give you money, a whole lot of money. . . ."

He was unable to complete his sentence because just then Agoak drove his knife through the man's skull, killing him instantly. His companion, who was still naked below the waist, lay panting and writhing pathetically on the kitchen floor. Agoak sliced off his penis

with one stroke of his blade. The man let out a terrible, inhuman
scream, a sound filled with the most atrocious fear and pain. Then
Agoak finished him off.

Without a moment's hesitation he cut off the other man's penis and
hurled it to the ground. Then he fell to his knees and began to cry.
Judith, who was slumped against the wall, was crying as well. Her
face was contorted and her whole body trembled. A low, whimpering
sound such as a wounded animal might make issued from the back of
her throat. Her hands opened and closed in a series of spasmodic
movements.

They remained in this position for some time. When the initial
shock had passed, it was Judith who rose from the floor first. She
had calmed somewhat, but her lips were pinched and her eyes hollow.
She picked her way over to Agoak, who was rocking back and forth
with his arms swaying at his side, his hands covered in blood. He
looked dazed.

The two bodies lay in a heap on the floor, butchered beyond
recognition. Scattered about everywhere were bits of clothing and
human flesh which had been hacked from the victims during Agoak's
savage attack with the knife, while not far from the window lay the
two bloodied penises.

Judith took Agoak by the arm, helped him up and led him to the
kitchen table. She pulled out a chair and sat him down before saying,
"I'll make some fresh tea."

Nothing stirred in Frobisher; the house was absolutely still as well.
Agoak slowly took in what was around him. He twitched a few times
and put his head in his hands. He sat there for a while as Judith just
stood staring at the white wall behind him.

By and by the water began to sing in the electric kettle, until the
sound changed into a quiet burbling. That seemed to be enough to
break the tension. Agoak raised his head and Judith put some tea in
the pot. As she was pouring the boiling water, Agoak said in a very
grave voice, "It's done."

Judith turned around sharply. Agoak repeated what he had said in
the same tone and motioned half-heartedly with his hands.

"It's done, everything's ruined. We're finished. . . ."

Judith had moistened a cloth and was busy sponging the blood
from her cut lip and injured nose, as well as from the long gash she
had over her cheekbone.

Agoak pushed back his chair and got up. He stood beside the two
bodies with his hands in his pockets and contemplated his deed.

"What are we going to do?" asked Judith.

"Head north," replied Agoak.

"What?"

"Make a getaway. Go north to the top of Baffin Island, as far as Ellesmere if we have to."

"How will we live?"

"The way the others do, the way our ancestors did before us."

"Agoak!"

"Do you think we have any choice? I've killed two Whites, two rich Whites at that."

"Do you know who they were?"

"Now I do, yes. I saw them and got curious. It wasn't hard to get the information. The control tower talked to Dorval to find out who the two of them might be. They're rich Americans. They cause trouble everywhere they go. Even here, as you can see."

"What now, Agoak?"

He stretched out his hands and announced in his mournful tone, "I killed them. All I can do is flee."

Then he threw back his shoulders, assumed a resolute and determined expression and said to Judith, "You'll have to give me a hand getting everything ready."

PART TWO

THE INUIT

CHAPTER I

Until the previous day, Agoak, who was handling the first sled, had left the problem of finding the sea to the intuition of his lead dog. As it happened, they had been more or less skirting the ice for some time. Since Agoak did not have much of a sense of direction, he had pretty well allowed the dog to find its own way, on the assumption that it had a well-developed instinct for self-preservation and that its needs and man's were closely intertwined. Before long the lead dog did find the sea, and in three day's time Agoak and Judith had killed two seals. It was Judith who gutted the first one, as Agoak stood by and watched, his feelings of nausea overshadowed by the imperatives of survival. As Judith was finishing, his resistance broke and he knelt down and cut the last tendon himself. After they killed the second seal, Agoak simply pushed Judith aside and without uttering a word, took sole charge of it. He thought of the lonely struggle that awaited them and, with his disgust in abeyance, he set about flensing the seal, removing the meat, cutting the fat up into blocks and putting the skin aside for Judith to make clothes from. Their physical survival was now assured for a little while.

As the dog-teams rushed headlong towards the North, Agoak paid closer and closer attention to the lay of the land, and kept a particularly watchful eye out for the rising shoreline that would tell him they were nearing the Cumberland Sea. At one point he thought he detected a slight hump in the ground, but it was difficult to make anything out on the eastern horizon because of the quality of the polar light. He would have preferred having a clear sky and a full moon — and a better idea of how to read the silhouette of the landscape. For it was essential that they move away from the coast and head for less inhabited regions. Then Agoak's caravan would be a

101

mere speck on the snow and would run little risk of being spotted from the air by a patrol plane. But what would happen come summer?

All of a sudden, Agoak stopped his sled and climbed off. There, crossing the dogs' path at an angle, was a set of tracks. He went over to examine them. The depressions were large and belonged to some massive creature. He quickly deduced there was only one animal which could have been responsible — a polar bear.

Agoak and Judith studied the tracks for some time. The bear had been moving quite slowly.

"All I know is what I've been told," said Judith. "It's lucky I remember." She pointed to the ground. "Look over here, and here. You can see how the claws have marked the snow. Look at the length of the stride. If he'd been running his paws would have been pointed inwards, because of the way he rolls from side to side. No, he's just taking his time."

"The tracks look fresh to me," said Agoak.

Judith nodded her head in agreement.

"Is he worth the trouble?" asked Agoak.

"There's the skin. And lots of fat for the dogs."

"And for us."

"Yes."

Judith started walking back to her sled.

"Do as you like," she said.

Agoak hesitated a moment, then placed his lead-dog's muzzle in one of the paw-prints and whispered words of encouragement in his ear. The dog swerved off in one direction, then darted back and forth sniffing carefully at the prints in the snow. Finally, after a few false starts, he headed off in pursuit of his quarry.

Late in the day, the dog stopped and made a whining sound. Judith reined in her team and came over to have a word with Agoak.

"I think he smells the bear nearby," she said. "See if you can spot him."

The two of them stood with their eyes narrowed to slits and their rifles at the ready as they surveyed the landscape. Agoak spotted an indistinct shape moving in the distance and he pointed his rifle at it. The creature was hard to make out, but after he moved around some more, there was little doubt as to who he was. He was atop a snow-dune, silhouetted against the sky, and, from the way he was glancing behind him, seemed to be on the alert.

"I'm going to get closer so I can take a shot at him," said Agoak.

Judith touched her husband's forearm.

"You can't afford to miss, you know."

"I know."

"He'll charge and try to kill us."

"I know."

She put her hand on his weapon.

"Shoot well," she said.

Agoak set off, as quiet as a cloud, walking with slow, measured steps. The bear now seemed less concerned. Everything was in Agoak's favor — the wind, the twilight, his own stealth. When he was within range, he brought his rifle very slowly up to his cheek, framed the bear's head in his sights and fired. At that very instant, Judith, who was positioned behind Agoak, fired her own high-caliber bullet. One of the two projectiles was right on target, for the bear reared up, beat the air with his front paws and then fell in a heap on the snow.

"I didn't need your help!" Agoak hissed at his wife.

He stomped back to his sled in a rage. Judith seemed taken aback for a moment, then regained her composure. She shrugged and got her dogs moving again. They fell in behind Agoak's sled and in a few moments they had reached the carcass.

"I'll take care of it," said Agoak.

Judith stood by and watched him. The thought occurred to her that less than a month had gone by and yet her husband was a changed man. She then reminded herself that she too had changed — but how could it have been otherwise?

Once the bear had been skinned and the meat and fat loaded onto the sleds, Agoak sized up what the spoils represented in terms of provisions for the future. He looked satisfied.

"The snow is good here," he said. "Let's make our igloo."

While Agoak cut the blocks of snow, Judith used her rifle butt to hollow out a trench and began placing the blocks in it. Working in conjunction like this, they managed to build the igloo in half an hour. Agoak looked after the entrance-tunnel, while Judith cut an air-hole in the centre of the roof. At the very beginning of their journey, Judith had pointed out to Agoak that as a child she had amused herself by building hundreds of igloos and was therefore good at it. She had soon proved herself right and Agoak had nothing but admiration for her. They had developed a routine in this way and now Agoak took it for granted that Judith would look after building the spiral dome herself and do it with such skill, that their safety and comfort would always be assured, no matter what calamities of weather were unleashed on them.

When the igloo was finished, they took what food and provisions they needed from the two sleds. The only light inside was cast by a single lamp, consisting of a flat earthenware dish filled with seal fat and a wick which burned with an unsteady flame. Judith got the metal tripod out of their belongings, set it up over the flame and suspended the snow-melting pan from it. Later, when the water was hot enough, she would make some tea and then use this meagre heat source to take the chill off a little of their meat. They ate in silence, chewing their food well. Huddled together as they were, staring blankly into space, they felt like two insignificant specks in the vastness all around them.

"I think I'm going to sleep," said Judith after swallowing a last mouthful. She took the skins they had brought in and threw them over the bench which hugged the wall of the igloo, then lay down with a groan. Agoak followed suit. He stretched out with his feet by Judith's head, muttering a string of unintelligible sounds and slipped into unconsciousness.

Outside, the dogs, who had feasted on the bear's innards, hollowed out a nest for themselves and settled down for a night's sleep. By and by, all was peace and quiet again on the eternal snow.

CHAPTER II

The evening of the murders, Agoak kept a remarkably cool head as he made plans for their escape.

Now that the whole structure of their lives had suddenly collapsed and there remained only the terrible reality of two mutilated corpses, their initial shock gave way to a growing realization of the enormity of the crime. Agoak weighed all the possibilities. Would he, as a native, ever be able to explain away having killed two rich White tourists? Not to mention having mutilated them, thought Agoak to himself, as he stared at the scene of slaughter for which he was responsible. There was only one thing to do: flee as soon, and as far, as possible.

Agoak nevertheless gave careful thought to the best way to proceed. First of all, it was barely six o'clock, still early evening. The streets would be fairly busy until at least ten o'clock. After that, the townspeople of Frobisher would gradually start heading for bed. Midnight would be a good time. They needed to get things ready, then wait until the town was settled in for the night. And take a chance on having someone knock at the door? As this was a distinct possibility, Agoak quickly pulled the two bodies into the bedroom.

"What about the blood on the floor?" asked Judith.

Agoak had a ready answer.

"We'll just say we got given another big piece of seal meat. You butchered it on the floor before putting it in the freezer. That'll have to do."

Agoak went back into the bedroom and, as he tried to avoid looking at his victims' remains, went through the chest of drawers, where he found some clothing. In the closet were several seal skins and two bear skins. He laid them on the floor, then went to the freezer, got out the meat they had stored there and placed it in the skins. He used thick leather belts to tie the meat into bundles. On Agoak's orders, Judith ransacked the cupboards for other foodstuffs, including a large quantity of tea which, fortunately, they had purchased on Saturday along with the other provisions. All in all, they weren't too badly off. Still, Judith, wanting to be prepared for any eventuality, had an idea. Envisaging the hard times which might be in store, she made a selection of kitchen equipment and utensils. It was difficult to imagine that any Inuk past or present could have been so well outfitted for such a trek.

"I'm finished what I have to do," said Judith, as she bumped into her husband.

She too had made up her own bundle using one of the skins. When they took stock, they found they had packed much more than they had expected. They were taking with them enough frozen meat for two weeks or more.

"Now we'll have to sit and wait," said Agoak.

The bundles were in the bedroom with the corpses. Agoak switched on the TV, but neither he nor Judith paid it much attention. At eleven o'clock, Agoak opened the front door, went outside for a moment to have a look around, noticed the town was already quite peaceful and went back into the house.

"A little while longer," he said as he sat down.

Midnight came and Agoak got up abruptly. Apart from the dogs yapping away nearby, everything was peace and quiet in Frobisher. He went out again, raced a few houses down the street, then returned a moment later leading two dog teams. The dogs, who were happy to be harnessed up and moving about, were quiet now.

"Let's get this done fast," said Agoak under his breath, "before anyone realizes we've got the dogs here."

They were almost running as they carried the bundles out from the bedroom. Agoak stayed behind in the house for a moment, to see if he'd forgotten anything. He ran through the list in his head: the frozen meat, the rest of the food, the clothes, the guns, the ammo, the kitchenware. They had everything they really needed. He closed the door gently, locked it and climbed aboard the first sled, while Judith picked up the reins of the other.

"Mush! Mush!" said Agoak to his dogs, and the caravan moved off, soon to disappear into the hills behind Frobisher.

The next day, some of their friends, who had begun to worry about Agoak and Judith, came to the house and someone finally broke down the door, only to find the two bodies. There was no denying the evidence: Agoak had killed two men, mutilated them horribly and then vanished, taking Judith with him.

Everyone in Frobisher was thunderstruck by the news. For many of the administrators and officials, Agoak had been the living proof of what an Eskimo could accomplish if he got off to the right start. Was he actually a killer? Had he really maimed and tortured his victims as well as killed them? It was as if a huge blissful cloud of gold and pink had suddenly burst and unleashed a cataclysmic storm.

Had he really killed two men, butchered them alive, cut off their penises — then left their remains and fled with two stolen dog teams? This bore so little resemblance to the Agoak people knew that it took many of them weeks to come to terms with the event and finally face the fact of Agoak's responsibility.

Meanwhile, an inquest had been completed and the RCMP organized a search team to go looking for Agoak. But the Arctic wind quickly obliterates all tracks and the polar light does little to help make a manhunt easier. It would be better to wait for the long, clear days of summer and organize flights over the possible escape routes. Although the good weather was still a long way off, the commanding officer of the Frobisher post had already marked some of these routes on detailed maps of the North. He was taking into account not only Agoak's distinct lack of experience, but also his intelligence and shrewdness.

"He'll stay close to the sea for the winter," went the officer's analysis, "but as soon as possible he'll start to veer off into the interior, in order to spend the summer there. He doesn't have either the experience or the stamina to get very far. He's going to lose his bearings completely somewhere around the Barnes Glacier. . . ."

The reasoning was sound, but didn't make enough allowance for the fact that Agoak's wiliness, coupled with the stimulating effects of fear, would make him a much more elusive quarry than the police imagined. Agoak pushed the dogs extremely hard as they crossed the interior, in the hope of getting to Ellesmere Island before the summer and then disappearing.

CHAPTER III

Agoak knew something about reading a map and had taken advantage of a clear night sky to observe the stars and plot his route. They had travelled alongside the glacier, which remained hidden in the twilight. Then one day Agoak spotted some breathing holes and, on closer inspection, some *agloos*. He knew they had reached the sea, and, with the next spell of clear weather, he realized he had brought them along the right course. At that very moment they were crossing the Straits of Lancaster. Before long they would be on Devon Island, then, after crossing Grise Fiord, they would reach Ellesmere and its mountains, where they could disappear for the duration of the summer.

Agoak kept driving the dogs. That evening, in the still of the igloo, he said to Judith, "Soon we'll be able to breathe easier."

They spoke little: above all, they had not exchanged a word about the murders since the night they left Frobisher. Agoak plotted their escape route, made the decisions and broke trail. Judith contributed to the effort her own expertise, her muscle power — for she was not a delicate girl — and whatever patience she could muster.

Agoak's attitude had changed overnight from that of a civilized Eskimo to that of a traditional Inuk who takes nothing for granted, cultivates his instincts and survives by his wits. The food they had brought lasted only three weeks. Fortunately, while stealing the dogs, Agoak had also stumbled on a good supply of frozen fish sitting carefully wrapped in seal-skins on each sled. There had been enough to last two weeks. By the time it was used up, however, they had travelled far and were near the coastline. They moved out onto the ice and had no trouble catching a fresh supply of fish, one large enough to sustain them through the next leg of their journey. Later on,

Agoak found himself at the icy shores of Cape Hooper, where he stopped to do some more fishing and replenish their supplies. As they were also low on red meat, he and Judith killed three seals, which they butchered and piled up on the second sled.

In the igloo that evening Agoak was more talkative than usual.

"Once we've left Baffin Land, it'll be easier," he said.

Judith was crouched over, putting tea on to boil. They had eaten and, for once, had not gone straight to bed. There was a twinkle in Agoak's eye and a certain vitality in his movements.

"I think we're over the worst part," he said.

"But we're still on the run," said Judith.

"Yes."

"Do you think the road will end somewhere?"

"No."

"You're prepared to spend the rest of your life running across the Top of the World like this?"

"If I have to."

He studied Judith.

"Why do you ask?"

She shrugged her shoulders and said nothing.

"Others before us have lived their lives as we are," he said. "They managed to keep going, to have children. . . ."

"Yes, like I'm going to."

"Does the idea worry you?"

She shook her head, but her voice trembled as she replied, "No, it doesn't."

Agoak fell silent again and drank his hot tea in short, loud sips.

After a while, Judith muttered, "But they didn't have the police chasing them . . . Agoak, this isn't how you wanted to live."

Agoak simply nodded his head.

"If you hadn't killed . . ." she started to say. Agoak, who was crouched opposite her, moved like lightning. His hand shot out and caught Judith full in the face with a violent slap.

"Now go to sleep!" he said sharply.

The next day they started out again, without any further discussion. Judith helped Agoak load the sleds, then they each harnessed up their own dogs, still without exchanging a word. All along, ever since their departure from Frobisher, there had been this silent, almost instinctual division of labor. It was not, therefore, a morning so very different from other mornings, except in the way they avoided each other's glance. Judith looked dejected. Agoak worked energetically, his head lowered, his expression determined. They had camped on the ice, but they would probably reach the shore of the strait by the evening of the next day. Then they would be in new territory, Devon Island, though nothing would really change for them.

Now they were travelling over the ice where the waters of the strait went down perhaps 300 metres or more. When they reached the opposite shore, however, the landscape would appear to consist of nothing but snow dunes stretching to infinity. Certain irregularities indicated the presence of hills and valleys, but they were smothered beneath the layers of snow, driven, sculpted and worn smooth by the wind, in this land without horizon, without point of reference and, in appearance at least, without any sign of life.

But Agoak was not troubled. They would build up their provisions from the fiord and this time, after reaching land, would set up a cache in a low igloo, so that by shuttling back and forth, they could ensure they had supplies enough for the rest of the winter.

As far as the summer was concerned, Agoak had plans in mind, but said nothing about them to Judith. In fact, talking with her was becoming rather difficult. Agoak mulled things over as he led his dogs across the smooth, unbroken surface. Agoak was a sensible man and had always been brutally honest with himself. It was a quality which had served him well over the years and continued to do so. He had fled because the only alternative was life imprisonment. A man of the outdoors, even if he had forsaken the old traditions, he now had no other choice but to let deeply buried instincts rise to the surface, to let himself be guided by them and in the end to adopt a way of life which, though it was not entirely alien, yet was not altogether the destiny he had intended for himself.

It took several weeks before he realized he had slipped from the one state into the other virtually without effort. So far he had managed to take each new problem in stride, thanks in large measure to the highly developed mathematical faculty which had been the basis for his success in the past. Yet he could not help but notice that as his hereditary link with the secrets of the Arctic came to the fore again, his identity as Agoak the computer expert was slipping away and he felt himself returning slowly but surely to the mentality of the Stone Age.

One result of this was that Judith was beginning to take on a new and altogether different dimension. Agoak now saw her primarily as a source of muscle power, a vital link in the effort to survive. He often wondered, as he pondered all this, just how it was that the attentive, loving husband in him had become the domineering male. Did it boil down to a question of survival? He believed it did and so decided to put it out of his mind once and for all. It seemed to him entirely justifiable that he punish Judith for any offensive remarks she might make.

At the same time, Judith herself was feeling strange stirrings, which seemed to have developed into a pattern over the period from the evening of the murders to the day Agoak had slapped her in the face. She called to mind the first few days of their journey. What astonished her was the feeling of having left behind everything represented by Frobisher and by her life with Agoak, the respectable, hard-working employee of the White man's bank, not to mention the delights of love or her work as a waitress. All this had given way to being forced to walk submissively behind her husband, to obey him and, if necessary, suffer punishment.

Had Judith, the sometime White woman, become an Inuk? Was it really true of her? She thought of Agoak, who had progressed from the status of bogus White man to that of a nomad on the very edge of survival! Even he, finally, was an Inuk. And now they moved forward laboriously in single file, looking spent and resigned and forlorn. Would they remain Inuit till the end of their days?

A good distance further on, after they had stopped for the evening, Agoak unfolded the large map of the Arctic he carried in his pack and, in the feeble light of the oil-lamp, proceeded to study the contours of the land round about. He took his time pouring over the details, then with a pensive look slowly folded the precious map up again and placed it on the ground beside him.

"See that you burn it before we leave in the morning," he said to Judith.

"Why?" she exclaimed.

"I can trust my own instincts better."

Judith recovered from the shock as fast as it had come upon her.

"As you wish," she said, forced to trust that he was right.

In the days that followed, Agoak made his way no less well for having fallen back entirely on his own intuition. Without being able to explain exactly why, he knew just when to veer off to the left, when to bear right, how to keep the dogs on track at all times. He was aware that he had come to resemble the traditional Eskimos who, for thousands of years, have relied on nothing more than gut instinct to assess the lay of the land they inhabit.

Agoak had no difficulty finding the large fiord where they would make their final stop for provisions before the coming of the thaw and the long days of summer. They spent several days crossing it before they were finally able to make out the rougher features of the shoreline.

"We're over shallow water here," said Judith. "There'll be both fish and seal. We should stop before we reach shore. In fact, we could even retrace our steps. We need to be quite far out."

They stopped for longer than usual this time and built a large igloo which was more a base camp than a temporary shelter. They then set about creating their food cache. This would be located closer to the shore, which would allow them to stay in the vicinity of their camp and catch their breath.

Once the igloo was set up, Judith took her rifle and went off to explore two agloos she had spotted earlier. Agoak caught up with her.

"Not today," he said. "We'll hunt tomorrow."

"There isn't much time."

"Tomorrow."

"Fine," she nodded.

They settled into the igloo early. As it was broader and higher, they were able to put two wicks in the stone lamp. It was therefore possible to boil more water at one time, and more quickly. It was almost luxurious.

Agoak, feeling more outgoing than he had in a long time, began thinking out loud, "I wonder what date it is."

"I can probably tell you in months," said Judith. She made a mental calculation. "Seven months, maybe eight."

"And I'm still a free man and we're still alive."

"Yes, I know."

He was lost in his own thoughts, and Judith felt the need to bring him back to earth.

"I have a way of calculating it," she said. "I try to work out from memory how many times we've had to catch fish to feed the dogs. One full load on the two sleds lasts about two weeks, maybe a little more. That comes to a good seven months according to my calculations, eight at the outside."

Agoak sat down next to her and, lifting her anorak, stroked her swollen belly. There was no mistaking the fact she was well advanced in her pregnancy.

"Your estimate sounds right," he said. "Eight months seems possible. You haven't got long."

"No."

The water began to simmer in the pan. Outside nothing stirred. The dogs, who were sated on frozen fish, were curled up for an early nap. Later on they would dig in for the night.

"Agoak," said Judith.

"Yes?"

He seemed surprised. There was a fervor in Judith's tone which brought back vague memories from a dim past he had almost put out of his mind. A reminder of other words, other sounds, another time, which seemed futile and unreal.

He shook his head violently.

"No!"

But she was already on him, her hands fumbling with his trousers, baring his sex, which was soon as stiff as a whip. Agoak tried unsuccessfully to push her away; the long months of travelling had made her a great deal stronger than before.

Suddenly nature had her way with them once more. Up to this point, they had been making love very little. By the time they settled into the igloo on any given night they were usually so exhausted, so drained by the enormous demands being made on them that they were rarely able to achieve union. And when they did, it was always without a sound being made. This evening, however, the atmosphere was more relaxed and Agoak could no longer hold back. He grabbed Judith roughly, tore her clothes off and, propping himself up on his hands to avoid her round, hard stomach, finally penetrated her. Their rhythm was gentle at first, then gradually became more frenzied. When Agoak's cries signalled the great exodus of sperm, Judith writhed about, crying and laughing at the same time. A series of powerful spasms swept through her stomach like so many waves rolling up onto a beach. Agoak soon recovered his composure and squatted on the ice bench, from where he watched Judith with a troubled expression. Judith was still catching her breath as she tried to put his mind at ease.

"It's not the baby — it just feels so good!"

They didn't quite fall asleep, but rather dozed off as they lay sprawled on their animal skins, while the water came slowly to the boil. When the curls of steam began to condense and freeze on the igloo walls, Judith got up and placed a good-sized portion of frozen seal meat in the water.

"We'll eat more tonight," she said. "We're here for a while. We've got big appetites and for once the meat'll be really cooked."

She adjusted the wicks in order to get more flame. When the water came to the boil a second time, Judith let out a little grunt of satisfaction.

"I'll let it cook properly if you don't mind waiting a little while, Agoak."

"I'll wait," he said.

"So long ago . . ." Judith muttered. "For everything. . . ."

Agoak didn't respond. His thoughts were elsewhere as he lay on the ice-bench naked under a polar-bear skin.

By and by they ate. Agoak chewed his food with obvious relish, savoring the juices in every mouthful, swallowing greedily and belching contentedly. He now seemed completely distracted. His mood was one of dejection, yet his face was utterly expressionless. He had a vacant stare, a lost look in his eyes, as though his mind were devoid of all thought, reduced to the level of an animal whose only concern is building up its strength again. Judith ate just as ravenously, though her eyes were brighter and her expression was more animate as she chewed her food and kept a close watch on her husband.

Soon Agoak began to slow the pace and take more time with each mouthful. After lingering over a last morsel, he let his hands drop and half-closed his eyes.

"I enjoyed that too," said Judith. "It was good."

Agoak still had nothing to say in reply, so Judith ventured another observation.

"Back at home the meat would have been cooked in the oven and served with vegetables. And there would have been dessert too."

Agoak sat up abruptly and howled with rage.

"Do you want to go back there?!"

"That's not what I said."

"If you want to go to jail, go back to Frobisher, go on, I won't stop you!"

Judith fell silent again and just stared at the ground in a posture of defeat. The water boiled in the pan and the oil in the wicks crackled. This was the only sound to be heard. Outside, the wind had subsided and the endless snow lay serene under a starry sky. The firmament was alive with constellations large and small, the eternal eyes of unknowable worlds, whose twinkling light could be seen reflected on the Arctic snows. Agoak and Judith, however, were oblivious to any such natural splendors. Agoak picked himself up, stretched out on the hard-packed snow of the bench and wrapped himself in skins in preparation for a night's sleep.

As Judith studied him, her mind was in a whirl and her heart in great distress. She set a bowl afloat on the boiling water, put some seal fat into it and waited motionless while it melted. Feeling limp and with a look of dejection in her eyes, she deliberately avoided thinking of anything, but instead concentrated all her attention on the fat as it slowly liquified. Once the bowl was full of the runny, yellowish and rather foul-smelling substance, she poured it into the stone lamp, holding back the unmelted piece with her finger. This would assure them of a minimum of heat and light as they slept. She stayed as she was for a moment longer, checking to see if there was anything else that needed doing, then finally got up and went to lie down in her usual place on the bench, where she curled up under a pile of skins with one hand placed on her swollen stomach.

While a glorious aurora borealis glimmered outside, Agoak and Judith, feeling gorged and exhausted, fell into a deep sleep in the igloo. They were travellers on a journey without end and slept without dreams or sensations of any kind, as though they had been swallowed up into a deep black abyss.

The next morning, in the clear light of day, Agoak said, "I'm going to take advantage of the good visibility to go back across the ice on the strait, for a good half-hour at least. I'll zigzag back and forth as I return in order to check for all the agloos I possibly can."

He left, while Judith stayed behind to keep an eye on the two agloos nearby and check for any signs of breathing. She seemed to lose track of the time, because she thought Agoak had been gone more than an hour when she saw him heading back. He had said something about zigzagging back, yet he was driving his dogs in a frenzied fashion straight for the igloo. He was badly out of breath when he pulled up.

"Plans have changed," he said.

"Why?"

"The police."

Her heart began pounding uncontrollably and she felt a strange sense of relief mixed with panic.

"Are they here?"

"They may be."

"They didn't see you?"

"No."

"What about our tracks?"

"The wind has blown away yesterday's tracks," he said. "But today's are still visible and there's no wind," he added in a tone of concern.

"How do you know it's the police?"

"They were camped about six miles from here. They left this morning and were headed North. I know what they'll do. They'll follow the shore-line, on the assumption I have to stick close to the sea in order to get food supplies."

"What are we going to do?"

"First of all, some fishing and hunting, then we'll leave, but not in the direction of the coast — back onto the strait."

Judith said nothing, but instead fetched a knife and a rifle.

"Let's go," she said, feeling calm once again.

Agoak had only to play his role as the man well. She was acquiescent; her role was to obey. Even she was surprised to feel so passive in her reactions. But there was nothing she could do to change. This passivity, this fatalism, was the ancient legacy of the Inuit women. What good was there in protesting it? Things would go on much the same as ever, no matter what one attempted to do. That's the way things were.

They set about their tasks with a vengeance. There was no question now of building up provisions for a cache. The proximity of the police had changed everything.

"Enough seal to fill what space we have," said Agoak, "and enough fish for the dogs to survive on, and no more. We can't overload the sleds."

They were busy all day long with their fishing and seal-hunting. Once or twice Judith spotted a school of small fish moving about in the water and regretted not having a net to catch some with, so that she could prepare a different sort of meal as a change from the steady diet of red meat. As it was, only the dogs ever got to taste fish.

That night in the igloo, Judith had a question.

"All you saw were tracks. How do you know it was the police?"

"Because there were two very big snowmobiles, pulling sleds."

They slept badly that night. Before they had been alert to the danger without really believing in it, whereas all of a sudden it was no longer a vague threat, but a concrete one, in the form of their pursuers. The police were there, and unless Agoak could find some way to outwit them, it was only a matter of time before they caught up.

They left in the morning and, as Agoak had planned, they headed out over the ice and away from the shore. The police had him sized up wrong if they thought he was going to behave in a predictable fashion.

Before they left, Judith said to Agoak, "It would have been better not to have burned your map. Especially now."

He whipped around towards her and said, "I don't need a map now and I never will!"

Judith, looking sulky, climbed aboard her sled and waited for Agoak to give the starting signal.

His plan was simple. And because it was unpredictable, their chances of success were good — at least for the time being. Agoak intended to take advantage of the last vestiges of winter to travel over the ice the length of Grise Fiord, put in a day on Coburg Island, continue skirting Ellesmere and head back to land near the mountains, well before Alexandra Fiord. He could have proceeded in the opposite direction, finding true north by the stars and sticking to the rear of Ellesmere Island. But that would have meant crossing the Devil's Gate, where the going was difficult and the lay of the land confusing. The itinerary he had chosen was longer, but less risky. He would avoid the coast and its uneven features as long as possible. Finally, if all went well, Agoak would turn hard to the left and, taking his bearings from that most important star, head right for the interior of the island. The last leg would take them to the mountainous massif, where human visitors were few and far between. By then the thaw would be setting in and they would be on the look-out for a well-concealed cave to shelter in for as long as was necessary. The game was plentiful and quite accessible which meant they would be able to build up their strength again, as well as dry themselves some caribou meat, ptarmigan and fish, and perhaps even spend the following winter in that same cave. The chances were, in fact, that they just might never leave, for they would be in seclusion, well off the beaten track. With a little luck, this scheme could be their salvation. But they had to hurry and get from the ice onto land before the start of the good weather, all without leaving tracks for the police to find. It was imperative they do so quickly, as quickly as possible, if they were to outwit and outstrip the police.

Agoak whipped the dogs, cursed at them, pushed them to their very limits. The remaining distance had to be conquered as though it were a mortal enemy. This was no longer an aimless journey undertaken without their knowing whether the police had begun to give chase. There was only one hope now and that lay in a race against time, which they would have to win . . . or else lose forever. It was a race which could only be won by sustaining the effort through each and every moment, as Agoak bore in mind while he whipped his dogs. He could not tolerate any slackening of the pace, because this was quite simply a matter of life and death.

They ran and ran, never letting up. By the time Agoak and Judith had thrown together the igloo each evening, they were so tired they would end up eating their meat half-frozen. Sleep was upon them long before the tiny flame from the stone lamp had brought the water to a boil, and they fell into the black abyss the moment the last mouthful was down.

On the third evening, however, Agoak was restless and seemed troubled by something. After finishing his meat, he got up.

"I'm going to have a look outside."

He picked up his rifle, checked to see that his knife was in his belt and went out.

Judith watched him leave without budging or speaking, yet was unable to sleep. She sat in a crouch with one elbow propped against the sleeping bench, playing distractedly with a lock of hair, a dreamy look in her eyes. It occurred to her that she had not, in fact, washed her hair for quite some time. Or her face for that matter. Agoak, too, was all shiny with the accumulation of oily dirt. She wondered if she'd look as filthy as she imagined she would with her clothes off. She thought back to their bathroom in Frobisher, with the big, white tub she would often soak in after coming home from work, her eyes closed, filled with a sense of well-being. And the taps, for hot water, cold water, as much as one could wish, all that pure, clean water. Not to mention the delicious, even, all-enveloping central heating. . . .

Suddenly she gave a start and sat bolt upright. Up to this point she had felt passive, docile and resigned to whatever fate Agoak might decide for them. But suddenly she seemed to be experiencing a resurgence of feelings which she had been trying to fight back over the months. There had been no time for second thoughts once they were hopelessly implicated in murder, and Judith had had no choice but to fall in unquestioningly with her husband. But with the past well behind them, it was beginning to dawn on Judith that she had been reduced to the utter servility and docility of the traditional Eskimo woman. Judith had made this journey strictly for Agoak's sake, because of what he had done. It had now become clear, however, that this was no longer the same Agoak. Ever since that terrible evening in Frobisher when he butchered the two men, Judith had watched with growing horror while he underwent a transformation, as if by some sinister magic. The successful Inuk, the man with the promising future, had regressed to the state of the cruel and bloodthirsty savage.

The Agoak of former days had quite simply disappeared in the course of their journey, to be replaced by the sort of Inuk Judith was more than familiar with — limited, narrow-minded, out of touch with the immediate past and concerned with survival alone. He had no more time for conversation and had lost any capacity for affection. Even their love-making had become no more than fornication. Having once been so considerate, so gentle in his love-making, so concerned to bring joy to their couplings and so skillful at achieving their common purpose, Agoak now took his wife only to satisfy his basest needs — to evacuate sperm and relieve congestion of the testicles. Gone were the provocative looks, the breathless longings of foreplay. Everything had been reduced to the level of sheer bestiality.

Was this how he wanted his life to end, eating half-frozen seal and living on the run in hastily-constructed igloos, pursued by the police, hunted down like a rabid animal?

Judith suddenly felt completely lucid as she sat quietly and weighed the pros and cons of this frenzied determination of Agoak's to plunge ever deeper into the frozen North. She was now convinced that he would end up getting caught or else that his attempt to survive would fail and he would die — and take her with him.

What might happen, she wondered, if they gave themselves up to the police in Frobisher? He had committed homicide, but only in order to defend his wife. The real wrongdoing lay in the savage way he had killed his victims, more like a beast than a man seeking revenge. It was a factor that would weigh heavily in the balance. Yet time has a way of rounding off rough edges. Would people still be as horrified today? As a prisoner paying for his deed, Agoak would lose his freedom of movement, though he never had been very fond of the great outdoors anyway. Besides which, there would probably be a certain demand for his skills in prison. . . . Meanwhile, Judith mused, she would be prepared to wait for him.

As she pondered these thoughts, Judith became aware that something very serious had come to pass. How many times had she allowed herself to be brutalized, without even getting upset, without feeling the slightest desire to rebel? Anyone observing their daily life from the outside would be struck by the extent to which Judith had severed all ties with the past, by the extent to which she seemed happy to return to a life of misery, danger and back-breaking labor. Was this not how she really felt in her own mind? Apart from the occasional twinge of nostalgia this past while, had she not completely resigned herself to Agoak's brutal ways, to the dramatic changes in his character?

She clenched her fists.

"I've had enough!" she yelled at the top of her lungs in the smoky light of the igloo. "Enough of this wandering through ice and snow, of freezing and eating raw meat, of slaving like a beast of burden. Enough!"

All this while, Agoak had been shuffling along, rifle in hand, not really knowing what he was looking for. In the igloo he had been overcome by an urge to go outdoors onto the ice and look for something. He could have been out there to check on the possible presence of the police, but the idea was a far-fetched one. The pursuing officers were bound to stick to the coast and were unlikely to surmise that Agoak was out on the ice. They were certainly aware, in any case, that it was useless to search for tracks on the ice, as these were quickly obliterated by the strong sea winds. If Agoak did decide to return to land, then the steep rock formations of the jagged coastline would act to protect any tracks from the wind and the police would have a much easier time locating him. Even they would have to admit that at this stage their manhunt was merely a gesture — though it might succeed in keeping the murderous Inuk on the run. When the thaw came, however, he would be forced to return to land and pitch camp. The police helicopter would then have little trouble spotting him, provided he could be contained within a fairly limited area. Or so the police believed anyhow. Agoak, for his part, was determined not to make it easy for them.

Though all this was on the Inuk's mind as he moved unhurriedly into the night, he realized he was not, in fact, all that concerned about what the police might be up to, not yet anyhow. Why, then, was he out on the wind-swept ice and what had he come looking for? He had no conscious reason for being out there and might almost have been walking in his sleep. He had been comfortably settled in the igloo when some inner impulse had led him outside. . . .

Agoak stopped for a moment, sensing danger. He turned his head slowly and scrutinized his surroundings. A blustering wind whipped Agoak's face with needle-sharp particles of snow, which forced him to keep closing his eyes. He cursed the relentless weather and blinked continuously in an attempt to penetrate the clouds of snow. By and by there was a lull and he looked west. He neither saw nor heard the huge polar bear as it loomed up behind him, but became aware of his presence only when one great paw descended on his arm, lacerating his hand and hurling his rifle some fifty metres away.

Agoak jumped back just in time to avoid a second sweep of the paw. He was without his gun now, but still had the long, lethal hunting knife which he carried in his belt. Agoak had only one choice: he couldn't make a run for it, since the bear was much faster than he was, so he would be forced to stand and defend himself. With lightning speed, he pulled out his knife, saw the bear coming at him again, ducked and twisted to one side, and managed to avoid being struck. At the same time he thrust his knife deep into the bear's chest, in the vicinity of his heart. The bear was seized with a terrible fit of rage and swung around to find Agoak, who had slipped in behind the great beast. The bear, now on all fours so that he could move more efficiently, rushed headlong at Agoak. The Inuk waited for him, feeling a sudden sense of composure, dodged the first sweep of the paw, but was unable to prevent the bear's claws from slashing the side of his head. He planted his knife in the fatty part of the bear's neck and caused blood to spurt out. The bear became still more enraged, roared, thrashed about, snapped at the blood which was running from his mouth and staggered back and forth in an effort to keep his balance. He charged at Agoak once again and succeeded in mauling his shoulder, but in doing so allowed Agoak to stab his neck a second time and puncture a carotid artery. All Agoak had to do was survive the next few moments, since the bear could not last long while losing such large amounts of blood. The bear in his rage only made this worse by moving around in a frenzy and increasing the flow of blood from his wounds.

In no doubt now about the threat to his life, the bear lunged wildly at Agoak, both from a standing position and on all fours. Agoak, fortunately, was small and very agile, and managed to keep jumping and feinting in a kind of macabre dance. Three times in succession he again went for the bear's neck and opened up the artery still more. Then, as the bear tried a feint to the left, Agoak was able to slash the other carotid artery and after spinning away skillfully, sank his blade home yet again. The bear's growl had now become a feeble groan. Suddenly he tried to lumber off, but Agoak leapt at him from one side and plunged his knife into the bear's head. Miraculously, the tip of the knife struck a cartilage rather than the bone of the skull itself, which would have bent or broken the blade before it penetrated to the brain. The bear, dead at last, keeled over on the spot. Seconds later Agoak himself collapsed and lay sprawled on the warm body of his conquered foe.

Back in the igloo, Judith had relived their fall from grace twenty times over. Detail by detail, image by image, she recreated the sequence of events from her childhood in Povungnituk to her present situation as Agoak's wife, as if spinning out threads and weaving them into a tapestry. Over and over again she called up memories of the most obscure vicissitudes of her life, focused her thoughts on Agoak's old self, on the way he had once been, and gradually, circumstance by circumstance, arrived at a consideration of how he had managed to sink so incredibly low. While she did so, she examined the interior of the igloo and compared it to the house she had lived in as a child in Povungnituk, as well as to the house in Frobisher they had been so brutally forced to abandon.

She examined too the impasse in which they now both found themselves. It was surely time for a return to reason, time to recover control of their destinies. She was just making up her mind that they simply could not go on living like this, when suddenly she heard the dogs start to bark. A moment later, Agoak slipped through the tunnel into the igloo. As he stood up Judith looked at him and let out a cry of horror.

Her husband was unrecognizable as it was, and if it hadn't been for the tough protective layer provided by his anorak hood, the bear's claws probably would have cut him completely to ribbons. Even a glancing blow from the bear's paw could do terrible damage. Agoak's head and shoulder were slashed almost right to the bone. He had made his way back to the igloo as best he could. He occasionally strayed off in the wrong direction as he did, but trusted his instinct to put him right again each time. At one or two points the pain and fatigue had slowed him to a crawl, and somewhere along the way he had dropped his rifle and had not had the strength to go back and look for it. Like a wounded animal, he had been only half-conscious and nearly delirious as he struggled along, groaning with the effort, and when he finally reached the igloo he was more dead than alive.

Judith helped him lie down on the fur-covered bench and looked him over. In former days Agoak's wounds would have paralyzed Judith with fright, but now she went to work assessing their seriousness and deciding what, against all odds, she could do about treating them. She would try to approach the task in a sober, dispassionate way. All there was in the way of medical supplies was what they had in the house the night they left, a few items Judith had hastily thrown into a plastic bag. They hadn't yet had occasion to use these supplies, so Judith had to go outside and find them in one of the bundles on the sled. It had been buried in so many layers of seal skin that none of the liquids had actually frozen.

She went back into the igloo and set about washing the coagulated blood from the gashes. Fortunately there was water boiling in the pan, which meant Judith could give the wounds a thorough cleansing before covering them with a thin layer of Vaseline.

Agoak remained fast asleep throughout the procedure. He had exceeded the limits of endurance, and all he could manage now was the occasional grimace whenever Judith came to a particularly deep wound. Once she was finished, he seemed to relax somewhat and after a moment, he turned over and curled up under the furs. Judith watched him briefly as she knelt at his side. She then spread a skin out on the ground close by, put some fat into the lamp to melt and took another wick out of her pocket, to add to the first. She went outside to get some snow, which she threw into the pan in order to maintain their supply of water. She then made tea in a series of calm, deliberate movements. She pushed the pan slightly to one side on the three-legged stand to make room for her tea, which she boiled in the Eskimo fashion. Finally, after filling her cup, she sat down heavily on the fur she had spread out, leaned against the sleeping bench with one elbow, the way she had earlier in the evening, and slowly savored the hot beverage, while in his deep sleep, Agoak started on the road to recovery.

CHAPTER IV

The days that followed were not easy ones. Because Agoak's diet had been so limited for the previous eight months, his body's stock of nutrients was badly depleted. Instead of healing, therefore, the wounds from the bear's claws became infected.

When he woke up the next morning, the wounds covering his head and shoulder were severely swollen, and it was obvious that infection had already set in. Agoak in his pain kept rolling his head back and forth, and seemed to be on the verge of delirium.

Judith, upset as she was by what she saw, tried to comfort him, but felt powerless to relieve his agony. She calculated, however, that it would do no harm for her to wash his wounds again with water as hot as he could stand, bandage them up and smear them with Vaseline, then make him take some aspirins. Agoak seemed soothed by this and went back to sleep. But it was a fitful sleep, interrupted by nightmares which caused him to babble incoherently. His forehead was ablaze and his body covered with sweat. In an attempt to raise the temperature inside the igloo a little, Judith melted some more fat and got four wicks going in the lamp. The water boiled more vigorously, and the humidity which this released into the air, along with the extra flames, made the igloo a little more comfortable. Finally, Judith sat down not far from Agoak and watched him to make sure he did not become uncovered, so that the heat from the furs would have the same soothing effect as her treatments.

Evening came and Agoak raved. He cried out occasionally, and much of what he said seemed to be connected with his computer work.

For part of the night, Judith was unable to sleep. During the day she had brought in a supply of snow for melting and kept the little four-wick fire going. She had also fed the dogs while outside and checked several agloos to be sure they were still in use. Since she was unsure how long Agoak might be confined, it was up to her to see they didn't run out of meat. By nightfall she was satisfied that everything was going as it should. Of course, there was still the police; but Judith had gone outside while Agoak was asleep and looked around carefully. She didn't mind admitting to herself that she would have been almost glad to see the black snowmobiles loom out of the distance. . . .

Something else troubled her: the polar bear carcass lying nearby. Agoak had described the encounter to her and now the bear's remains were lying unprotected in the open, at the mercy of other predators. There was meat and fat to be had, and, better yet, a big, warm, soft fur of the best quality, one which would suit Judith's needs perfectly. But how was she to retrieve it without having to leave Agoak to his own devices?

She didn't even bother lying down that evening, but simply fell asleep with her head leaning against the pile of furs, her face not far from Agoak's boots. She dreamt she was in some sunny land, wearing a light dress which revealed her breasts. On it were numerous speckled butterflies with big wings, which added to the alluring effect. In the vast sky behind, a radiant and angelic kind of music played in accompaniment to the silky song of gentle breezes, and Judith smiled in her sleep.

In the morning, Agoak's groans brought Judith back to grim reality. Inside this igloo, lost in the vast, icy wastes, a man was dying, and Judith was no longer even sure whether she wanted to save him. Without thinking about it, she sponged off Agoak's forehead, which was running with sweat, checked his wounds and saw that the infection seemed to have stabilized.

Judith turned things over in her mind as she sat at Agoak's feet drinking her first cup of tea, the one which now served as breakfast in place of the eggs and toast she had enjoyed in the not-too-distant past. It seemed to her that, the weather being as mild and clear as it was, she could put Agoak on one of the sleds and take him to the village of Grise Fiord, which she knew lay to the north-east.

She could probably save Agoak by doing so, since there was a hospital there. It occurred to her at the same time — though in an almost subconscious fashion — that she could save herself as well. How many days away could the village be? Two, three, maybe more. She could dispense with building an igloo at each stop-over. Agoak would be bundled up in furs; moreover, they still had the thermos bottle which had been rescued from the disaster in Frobisher and brought along just in case. By filling it with boiling tea she would have something warm to serve both the patient and herself. And heavens, if it became absolutely necessary to erect an igloo in order to replenish the tea or take the chill off a piece of seal meat, she would simply do it. As far as the dogs were concerned, short rest periods and double or triple portions of fish would surely allow them to keep up the pace without difficulty.

The plan was a good one. She would leave the other dogs behind to run free and fend for themselves. She would also abandon the extra food and supplies. Grise Fiord might actually mean journey's end for them. Never again would they be obliged to take to the icy tundra, or with the advent of summer, to the rocky, deserted islands of the North. Nothing would ever be the same again.

Naturally, it would mean prison. But the worst kind of prison would be paradise by comparison with the igloos, the blizzards, the dog-sleds and the eternal struggle for survival. The more she thought about it, the more resolved Judith became to see an end to their woes. There was a perfectly good pretext as well: saving Agoak's life.

She could contain herself no longer. Everything seemed clear, the implications of her decision, what had to be done to carry it out. She came back into the igloo after being outside a moment and quickly set about preparing tea for Agoak. He was in a stupor, panting with fever, and his eyes looked dead. Judith glanced at him momentarily, then leaned over, put her arm under his shoulders, raised him to a sitting position and managed to get him to drink a long gulp of tea while she held his head. He slumped back and Judith stayed by his side to keep an eye on him. It would be easy enough to bundle him up, because he was already lying on the big polar bear skin, on top of which were a very large caribou hide and two large seal-skins; besides that, he had never taken off his anorak. She would roll him up in the furs, put a balaklava cap over his head, pull up the hood and drag him outside. Then she would tie him firmly to the sled — and head for deliverance.

Inside the igloo the silence was broken only by Agoak's raspy breathing and the rustling of Judith's clothing. Judith checked to see that she was dressed properly and was satisfied she was ready to brave any weather, even the worst blizzard. She had looked over the dogs and they seemed in good shape. Before coming inside, she had served them large helpings of fish and loaded the sled with the

provisions they would need for the journey of several days to Grise
Fiord. Everything was ready.

She took a last gulp of tea, wrapped up the few supplies that had
found their way into the igloo and took them outside. When she got
back, she set about her task with determination. It was now or never.

She proceeded to wrap up Agoak, who was still only half-
conscious. Then she grabbed hold of him and began to drag him
towards the entrance-way. She had hardly gone three steps when
Agoak thundered at her, "What do you think you're doing?"

Judith stopped in her tracks and let go of him. Agoak quickly
extricated himself from the rolled-up hides and stood up. Was it
possible he had suddenly recovered from his fever? She could see he
was unsteady on his legs, but he wore a terrible expression of rage
which had twisted his lips into a snarl.

"Where were you taking me? Outside, to let me die?" he asked in a
voice rock-steady with anger.

"No, don't say that. I was trying to save you. I was going to take
you to the hospital at Grise Fiord."

"The hospital?"

"Yes, there's supposed to be a hospital there."

"There's something else in Grise Fiord too."

"What?"

"A Mountie post. Is that where you were taking me? . . . Well, was
it?"

"No!"

Dispensing with any further discussion Agoak began pummelling
Judith with his fists and feet. Crying and moaning, she tried to
defend herself as best she could, then took refuge on the bench, where
she buried her face in the pile of hides, while Agoak continued to
beat her.

Agoak's weakened condition finally got the better of him and he
too ended up collapsing on the bench, gasping for breath, his eyes
glassy and his face covered with sweat. Judith got up painfully. Her
forehead was split open, her eye swollen and her hand bruised. She
squatted down by the lamp and began rocking slowly backwards and
forwards, testing her injuries with one finger as she rocked.

She remained in this position for some time, feeling dazed and
distracted. She realized now that the fine dream she had had about
bringing their problems to an end in Grise Fiord was futile. Even on
the verge of death Agoak was capable of mustering self-protective
resources she could never overcome. In one burst of energy he was
quite capable of killing her.

Should she wait for him to die? He looked weak, but he was unlikely to die in the immediate future. She felt a chill of horror sweep through her. Was this really the man she had loved so much in Frobisher and before that in Povungnituk, who had once been so special, so loving? Was this the man she now wished death on? The sled and the dogs waited outside, but what use were they anymore?

The hours slipped by. She felt helpless, caught up in a situation from which there seemed to be no escape. Agoak, who even in his moribund condition had managed to beat Judith cruelly, began to regain consciousness again. He propped himself up on one elbow, took a look around and stared at Judith, who was obviously suffering from her injuries.

"Give me some tea," he said in a contemptuous tone.

He was still in the grip of the fever. He shivered and the sweat ran down his face. But he was moving more easily now and his voice had become steadier.

Judith got up, poured some tea into a cup and handed it to Agoak, all in a grudging fashion, without looking at him. He expressed no gratitude, but merely took the tea and gulped it down noisily, smacking his lips with satisfaction.

Judith sighed.

"Agoak," she said.

Agoak lifted his head and looked at her, but said nothing.

Judith resolved to pursue her point.

"The occasional 'thank you' would make things a lot different, Agoak."

He watched her impassively.

"If we could only talk the way we used to. We managed to get things across."

"We have nothing to talk about," said Agoak dryly. He leaned back and averted his glance. His expression was unyielding.

A shriek from Judith brought his attention back.

"Have you gone completely crazy? We've been on the run like hunted animals for eight months, eating seal and living in igloos. There've been weeks when we haven't exchanged a single word. You give your orders and I obey them. Have you forgotten the past completely? Just compare who you once were with who you've become."

"I do what I have to do."

"Oh really? What you have to do? Such as acting like a brute, talking to me the way you talk to your dogs? Or beating me if I don't get down on my knees and grovel? Or slapping me around if I dare have an opinion? Do you think that's what I married you for, what I came to Frobisher for?"

"I don't have any choice."

"Why not?"

"Because I killed two men."

"You killed them to protect me."

"I'm a murderer."

"And that explains why you beat me up and forget we were ever in love? All I am to you anymore is just another sled-dog."

Agoak shrugged his shoulders and turned away.

"Agoak, you can't keep running and hiding all your life. Once it might have been possible, but today it isn't. As soon as the good weather comes, the helicopters'll be out looking for us, and it'll only take them a few days to find us. You're very ill and you're going to need time to get better. We can't start running again. I wanted to take you to Grise Fiord so you could be looked after."

"Looked after by the Mounties."

"Agoak!"

"They'd look after you too."

"If it means going to jail, Agoak, too bad! Jail would be a thousand times better, for you as well as me, than racing across the tundra in a dog-sled, sleeping in a freezing igloo, eating seal and never knowing when and where it's going to end. At least in prison it's warm, there's food and we wouldn't have to run anymore."

Agoak cackled.

"So that's your plan, is it? Have me captured, so the two of us can rot away in some nasty prison?"

"I don't have a plan, Agoak. I just want the best for us. I want you to see reason. I came on this journey with you, no questions asked, believing we'd find a way out. I was sure something would work. The two of us weren't in any position to think it over at the time. We had to act and act fast. Later I wanted to make things easy for you, so I just took orders. You didn't talk to me, you didn't show me any love, but I was prepared to be patient. I never even got a smile from you. As a matter of fact, Agoak, how long has it been since you've laughed?"

"You think there's something to laugh about?"

"But would a smile hurt, Agoak, a little kindness? We're not living like human beings, Agoak, we're living the way our ancestors must have, hardly better than animals."

"Why don't you just leave me alone!"

"We used to be able to talk and laugh and have fun together. We were nice to each other. Look at us now. All we've done for months is exchange grunts, like animals. I had dreams in Povungnituk of what I wanted to do. I wanted to live in the Arctic, because I belong here. But I never wanted to go wandering over the ice, freeze in an igloo, gulp down frozen seal, run from any sign of human life, live in fear of the slightest noise — or get punched in the face by my husband."

"Why don't you just tell me what you want!" Agoak shouted.

"I want things to be like before."

"Things can never be like before! The past is over! All that matters now is staying alive from one day to the next, if it's remotely possible. There's nothing left of the past, nothing!"

"*We're* left, Agoak, here in the present. Even if the life we have to lead is hard, it would be a lot more tolerable if we lived it together and acted like two people who loved each other."

"Just shut up, will you? Do you hear me — shut up!"

But Judith only shook her head and groaned.

"Agoak, you don't understand!"

He came towards her with a menacing look. Judith tried to protect herself as the blows came raining down. He beat her until she collapsed in a heap, then threw himself onto the bench and fell asleep.

CHAPTER V

Judith woke up surprised to find herself lying on the fur she had laid out beside the ice bench while tending to Agoak. As lucidity returned, so did the memory of the previous night's beating. She could never remember feeling so upset before. She failed completely to understand what had happened to her husband. She had tried to have a serious, intelligent discussion and he had rejected any idea of their trying to communicate. And then beaten her. Fine, if that's the way it was to be, what was the point of making any attempt to understand each other? If he wanted to keep on living like an animal, he could do so. Only she wouldn't stick with him any longer. She would simply leave him. If he was capable of beating her black and blue, he could just as soon treat his own wounds. Judith had had enough.

Checking to see that Agoak was still fast asleep, she lifted the hood of her anorak, crouched down and slipped out through the entrance tunnel. Her mind was made up. She would flee on her own and keep going in the direction of Grise Fiord as long as she could. She had her rifle and ammunition with her, and was prepared to defend her life, whatever the cost. Better to perish than continue this life of misery, of beatings, of flight without hope, without end.

For a certain measure of love, tenderness and consideration, Judith was ready to go to the ends of the earth. But not for beatings and scornful silence. In three days, or with a little luck, perhaps even less, she could forget this nightmare forever and begin to live normally again. She was ready to take the decisive step.

With her rifle on her arm, Judith called quietly to the dogs, then harnessed up five of them and hitched them to the sled she had intended to carry Agoak on. Everything was ready and Judith was just adjusting her mittens when she happened to look up and saw shapes moving in the distance. At the same time she could hear the tell-tale yapping of dogs hauling a load. The police travelled on snow-mobiles: whoever was approaching, therefore, had to be Eskimo. She stood stock still, feeling terrified and relieved all at once. It was a stroke of fate.

Little by little, the shapes became clearer. From their movements and the way they handled the sled, there was no doubt they were Inuit. Judith waited. Suddenly she heard something behind her. It was Agoak coming out of the igloo.

The other Inuit got closer still. Agoak's voice indicated he had rapidly recovered much of his strength. It was resonant, as well as scornful.

"Who's that coming?" he wanted to know. He stood not far from Judith, his hood pulled up and his rifle under his arm, like Judith, watching the strangers draw near.

The twilight was clear enough for them to see that the Inuit had children with them, and three extra dogs, in addition to the two teams which were in harness.

"I wonder who it could be?" asked Judith in turn.

Agoak made a grunting noise in the back of his throat and said, "They're not welcome here. We don't need visitors."

"But you don't know who they are yet."

Agoak remained impassive as he kept his eyes riveted on the moving figures. When they were about fifty metres away and could see that Agoak and Judith were waiting for them, with guns at the ready, one of them cried out, "Inuk!"

Judith answered in the traditional way.

"Inuk!"

In principle, they had nothing to fear. The sled covered the last few metres of its journey and pulled up in front of them. The man shuffled slowly towards Agoak. His wife, who was right behind him, began walking in Judith's direction when there was a squeal of recognition from the two women.

"Mimi!"

"Judith!"

Agoak and the other Inuk wheeled around wearing a look of astonishment.

"They're the Inuit I met in the restaurant," Judith explained. "Do you remember?"

Agoak did remember. It was the day Judith had stormed out of the house and slammed the door behind her, the day she had him convinced that her preference was to see him revert to the nomadic life. Agoak looked the newcomers over and said to his wife in a facetious tone, "You see? We finally made it."

Judith said nothing in reply, and the other couple looked at them quizzically.

"Never mind," said Judith after a pause. "I'll explain later. His name is Kigugtak and his wife's name is Mimi," she added, turning to Agoak. She beckoned to the two children. "She's Lucy and this is Tomassee, the boy." Pointing to Mimi's hood, she said, "There's another boy named Imooshi in there. Is that right?" she asked, addressing Mimi.

"Yes," replied Mimi. "You have a good memory."

"I enjoyed meeting you. I always remember pleasant things better."

Once the preliminary niceties were over, however, the situation became somewhat uncomfortable. Judith didn't question whether the other couple might know about what had happened in Frobisher, for it was quite obvious they did. Kigugtak in particular was not doing a very good job of concealing how ill at ease he felt. It was Agoak who decided to clear the air.

"Has it been long since you were last in Frobisher?" he asked.

"Yes," replied Mimi. "We haven't been back since the time we met Judith."

"But we've just come from Grise Fiord," Kigugtak hastened to add.

"And news travels fast," commented Agoak in a calm voice.

"Yes," said Mimi.

"So you know about what I did?" said Agoak.

"Yes," said Mimi. "But they were raping Judith. You were right to kill them."

Kigugtak looked away and kept silent, as Agoak watched him.

"Maybe people thought I killed them too violently."

There was a pause.

"I don't have to explain what I did. I am the way I am."

"Come into the igloo," exclaimed Judith. "We've got some seal and there's water boiling. We can have some cooked."

"We have some caribou left over from a summer hunt," said Mimi. "Would you like some?"

"Oh yes!" said Judith.

They entered the shelter one by one. With all the children and the adults, the igloo was filled to capacity and soon warmed up nicely. They stretched out, relaxed and chatted while Mimi's piece of caribou thawed and cooked in the pan. The preliminary suspicions had disappeared and everyone now seemed to be getting on quite well. Kigugtak wore a friendlier expression and even Agoak, for all his hostility, had become more sociable. He looked pensive as he studied each of their guests in turn. Mimi and Judith had struck up a warm, intimate conversation almost immediately. They talked mainly about the children, and Judith showed off her stomach.

"Look," she said, "it's happening to me too."

Mimi's face beamed as she expressed how happy she was for Judith. Judith herself giggled with sheer joy.

"Were you getting sick at first?" asked Mimi.

"No, not at all, not for one moment."

"And you're keeping well?"

"Couldn't be better."

"It must be happening soon!"

"Yes."

"When?"

"I've lost track of the dates, I don't even know what month this is."

"It's May," said Mimi.

"Yes, then it will be soon."

"May," said Agoak, as though thinking out loud. "The month of May already."

"The day before yesterday we were in Grise Fiord and it was May 6," said Kigugtak.

"The day before yesterday?" asked Judith.

"Yes."

"We're quite close to the village then."

"Yes," said Kigugtak. "And we didn't push the dogs very hard either. It's really very close."

"May 6. We're not far from Grise Fiord and it's nearly time for the thaw."

"That's right," said Kigugtak. "Close to shore, it felt to me like the ice wasn't so hard."

"Already!" exclaimed Judith.

"It isn't ready to break up yet," said Kigugtak, "but it seems less solid. I'd say the snow was wetter too."

Agoak was lost in thought. He nodded his head back and forth and seemed to be busy muttering things to himself.

"The caribou's cooked," said Judith. "Look!"

She pulled some meat out of the pan. The children were served first, as is the Eskimo custom, and then each adult chose the piece he wanted. They had been eating for some time when finally Judith broke the silence.

"After nothing but seal to eat for eight months or more, caribou is awfully good."

Everyone agreed. And, surprisingly, it was Agoak who agreed most enthusiastically. A subtle change had come over the man. He had acted very aloof when their unexpected visitors first arrived, but then gradually became more talkative. For someone who had been so wrought up, he was now remarkably relaxed and expansive. It had been a long time since Judith had seen him in such a mood. And she wasn't sure she liked it. Because while Agoak may have had equally chatty moments in Frobisher, there was something different about the look in his eyes now, a shifty quality Judith didn't like at all. He peered at the clothes the other couple wore and the weapons they had brought into the igloo, and asked, "Has the hunting been good for you?"

"We were lucky," replied Kigugtak. "Just before the freeze-up we killed some caribou and made ourselves an ice cache at our camp, just below Pangnirtung. We've still got 45 kilos of it on the sleds."

"You certainly were lucky," said Agoak. "Have you had any problem finding seal?"

"No. There's seal everywhere. As long as we're on the ice, we never run short. But there'll be caribou and fish again when the summer comes."

Kigugtak was pleased at the thought and laughed softly.

"Life is hard in the winter, but things get better in the summer."

"It's more difficult to travel," said Agoak.

"Yes, but we get the things we need while there's still ice. Like this trip, our ammunition was getting low so I thought we'd better go to Grise Fiord and buy some. We've got 1500 cartridges on the sleds and about forty traps. When the thaw comes, we'll be back at our cache and have what we need to shoot and trap all we want."

The children were stretched out asleep on the bench. It was warm and quiet in the igloo.

"I noticed your wounds, Agoak. What happened to you?" asked Kigugtak.

"He fought a polar bear, a huge nanook," Judith replied for him.

"Fought?" said Kigugtak, with an intrigued look.

"The bear knocked his rifle away. He had to fight him with a knife."

Agoak had been sparing with the details, but he had said enough about the incident for Judith to appreciate the circumstances and implications of his face-to-face battle. From that point of view, she was very proud of her husband. It was an act of great courage, she had to admit. And one which others ought to hear about as well. It was not, of course, the first time an Inuk had been pitted against a nanook with only a knife for a weapon, but the event was rare enough that any Inuk who emerged victorious from such a confrontation was regarded as something of a hero. In any case, there was so little about their recent life that was heroic or about which they could be proud, that it was definitely a story worth telling.

Kigugtak looked admiringly at Agoak. Mimi similed proudly and made a kind of cooing sound as she looked at Judith.

"Nothing but a knife!" exclaimed Kigugtak.

"That's the only weapon I had left," said Agoak.

"And you finally killed him?"

"Yes, but he wounded me first."

"He was still very ill yesterday," said Judith. "You seem better now, Agoak."

He surprised Judith with a strange smile.

"For the time being," he said, "I'm much, much better."

A brief silence descended on the igloo. Something in Agoak's smile and the tone of his voice had left the visitors temporarily at a loss for words, without their really knowing why. To break the tension, Mimi said in a playful way, "He's better because he likes having visitors!"

"That could be it," said Agoak. "Yes, I'm sure that has a lot to do with it."

This time he spoke in a completely natural tone and even patted one of the sleeping children on the head.

"Did the bear damage your rifle?" asked Kigugtak. "He might have broken something when he knocked it out of your hands."

"I don't know. It's still out there in the snow. I was too badly injured to go looking for it. I just managed to drag myself back here."

"I thought he was finished when I first saw him," said Judith. "It was a terrible sight, the gashes, all the blood. . . ."

Kigugtak raised his hand and touched Agoak's worst wound, which ran down his head and into his cheek.

"It's hollow," he said. "That blow could have killed him."

"It's my hood that saved me. It got shredded in the process and it's barely usable now. Look."

He showed them what was left of the hood of his anorak.

"You're really lucky to be here with us today," said Kigugtak.

"You might never have come back."

"Yes, I suppose."

"I don't know of a single Inuk who's ever got away alive from a fight with a polar bear using just a knife," said Kigugtak.

"It's my own fault in a way," said Agoak quietly. "I don't know much about living the nomadic life. If I'd been more observant, I would have seen the bear in time. I should have been more careful with my gun too. I was holding it wrong, dangling it from my hand instead of carrying it tucked under my arm. The bear's paw swung right into it and sent it flying. It taught me a lesson."

"Was it windy?"

"Yes, and it was snowing heavily."

"When there's a blizzard it's best to stay in the igloo and wait," said Kigugtak with a shake of the head.

"I think I was fated to go out," said Agoak. "I felt like something was pushing me outside. I don't know why, but I just had to do it. I'm sure it was fate."

Suddenly he had taken the tone Judith was so bothered by. There was a kind of contained irony in it, as though he were enjoying some private joke which he did not intend to share with the others.

"Anyway, it's always fate, isn't it?" he added.

Once again it was Mimi who responded to the tension she saw written on Judith's face, while Judith herself was baffled by her own reaction. Twice now she had taken offence at this attitude of Agoak's, yet she was unable to imagine what might lie behind it. What surprised her most was that Agoak's burst of good humor was completely out of keeping with the way he had behaved since being wounded by the bear, and came hard on the heels of the terrible beating he had given her after discovering she had intended to take him to Grise Fiord.

A few hours earlier, as Kigugtak and his family arrived and Agoak stumbled out of the igloo, Judith had been standing beside a sled that was obviously packed and ready to leave. Agoak had spotted all the supplies on the sled at one glance and had the situation sized up before turning his attention to the newly-arrived strangers. He was intelligent enough to see that Judith had been about to run out on him while he slept. Was this the reason for his uncharacteristic sarcasm, now that everyone was in the igloo and he was playing at being the gracious, cordial host? She wanted to think so.

"Say, where's the bear you were talking about?" Mimi asked all of a sudden.

"He's still out there," said Judith. "Nobody's been able to go for him yet."

"And now it's too late," said Kigugtak. "He'll be frozen and there's nothing you can do about it. It's a nice catch to have left behind. There's the meat, the hide, the fat. . . ."

"Would it help if we made an ice cache?" asked Mimi.

"What would be left after the thaw?" asked Agoak.

They all looked at one another and felt vexed that there was a precious supply of food nearby which was of no use to them.

"We could always sacrifice the skin and take an ax to it," said Kigugtak. "That way we might salvage a few chunks of meat. . . ."

Agoak threw up his hands in a gesture of futility. But Mimi had a suggestion.

"Listen," she said, "I think we can do something about it. You men stay here. Judith and I will take a couple of axes and ride the sleds over to where the bear is. Even if we only get a little, that'll be something. Kigugtak is right, we'll just have to sacrifice the skin."

Kigugtak nodded his head affirmatively and looked at Agoak, waiting for his response. He was obviously thinking it over and something about it seemed to please him enormously, because he was grinning more and more broadly and had an unusual twinkle in his eye.

"Why not?" he said to Kigugtak. "If the women want to go to this trouble, let them." Then, still smiling ironically, he said to Judith, "You can split whatever you salvage between you."

Judith suddenly felt uneasy once again, hesitated for a moment, then shrugged her shoulders and pulled up her hood.

"Are you coming?" she said to Mimi.

"Yes."

Agoak raised his arm and pointed in a north-westerly direction.

"He's that way, a little over a kilometre from here."

Judith breathed easier once she was outside. She didn't confide any of her puzzlement about Agoak to Mimi. Instead she took in several deep breaths of the pure, clear Arctic air, being careful to keep her mouth closed so as not to injure her lungs, for it was cold enough to freeze the horns off a caribou that day. While Judith roused her dogs from a cozy sleep, Mimi went off to fetch one of her own dog-teams.

"This way," she pointed out, "if we do manage to get a good deal of meat, we'll have the two sleds to load it on. You see?" she added, "I have high hopes for us."

They had little trouble finding the bear's carcass. Fortunately, the wolves hadn't smelled it and had never come near it. Judith scouted the immediate vicinity and soon found the spot where Agoak's rifle had dropped into the snow. She quickly recovered the weapon and carried it back to the sled. Together she and Mimi checked to see that the action was still in working order. The magazine was full and there was no damage.

"That's one thing at least," said Judith.

"We're having a good day," said Mimi. "Both the rifle and the bear are in one piece."

Judith secured the gun on her sled and removed the ax which was permanently affixed to it. Mimi didn't seem in any hurry to get started on their task. She leaned against her sled and studied Judith.

"I wonder what's going on in your head, Judith," she said.

Judith looked quizzically back at her companion.

"Why?"

"When I met you in Frobisher you were upset because you thought your husband wanted to go to Toronto at any cost. You didn't think he was enough of an Eskimo."

"Yes. I found he was too quick to disown his origins, and I was afraid he might leave for the South."

"Would you have gone with him?"

"I've come with him this far."

"True."

"I would have gone South with him. That's all a woman can do, isn't it?"

Mimi nodded.

"How about you, Mimi? Do you like living the way you live?"

"Not all the time. Sometimes I feel really cold and hungry. I know what it's like to be in a real house. I lived in one once and I'd go back again."

"Me too," said Judith. "I'd go back. To any real house. Even to prison."

"Would they put you in prison if you went back?"

"Yes, I think they would."

"Really? But why?"

"For leaving with him, for not turning him in, for helping him. The law says that even the wife of a criminal can't help him escape."

"And you did."

"Yes, that's just it. But I'd almost be glad to go to prison. I'd accept almost anything if we could only stop running."

"You know, Judith, maybe I don't like everything about my life, but we are free, we're really free. We come and go as we wish, Kigugtak really knows how to organize things, so we don't lack for very much. The children are happy and in good health. . . . One day, of course, we'll go and live in an Eskimo settlement. In about three years, in fact, when it's time for the children to start school. And I know I'm eventually going to get fed up with the life we're leading at the moment."

"You must be made differently from me," said Judith. "I wouldn't ever get fed up with it."

"It can grow on you, I must admit."

"In Povungnituk, and even in Frobisher, I used to get a little envious when I saw people like you. You remember the time I met you, I had had an argument with Agoak when you and Kigugtak drove past the house on your sleds. Then I went to the restaurant and talked with you, remember?"

"Certainly, I remember, I found you very pleasant to be with."

"And I kept badgering you with questions. Funny, I talked about the nomadic life in a nostalgic sort of way, even though I'd never lived as a nomad. I'd already made up my mind I was going to like it. . . . And now, as you can see, I don't have any choice in the matter."

"Do you think you can last, Judith?"

"No, I don't," Judith replied, shaking her head.

"What're you going to do?"

"I don't know."

"Do you think you'll leave?"

Judith threw up her hands.

"Leave? How can I? You don't think I'd ever manage to sneak out of the igloo while he was sleeping, do you? With the racket the dogs make as soon as they're hitched up! Even if Agoak was fast asleep, that would be enough to waken him up."

"I want to help you," said Mimi.

"There isn't much you can do. Agoak has become a brute. And he's stronger than I ever would've imagined."

"I have an idea," said Mimi, "and I think it may solve your problem for you. When I was in Frobisher, I went to the clinic and had some sleeping pills prescribed for me. You see, I have trouble sleeping, and I need all the rest I can get, after the kind of day I put in and with the kids and everything. I can let you have some of the pills. They'll knock him right out."

"But how can I get him to take them?"

"You can tell him I gave you some pills for the fever and the infection. . . . In fact, I can tell him myself when we get back to the igloo. I'll give Kigugtak a wink and he'll figure out something's going on and keep quiet."

"Agoak's not very gullible. . . ."

"You can always dissolve some in his tea. He drinks it strong and boiling hot, so it'll hardly change the taste."

"Do you think it'll work?"

"Yes, I do."

"He'd kill me if he found out."

"It'll work, you'll see. I'll also ask Kigugtak not to travel too far. We can go back the way we came and wait for you. When you catch up to us, we'll drive the dogs back to Grise Fiord at top speed. Once you're back, you'll be safe."

"And Agoak will fend for himself."

"He'll have to."

"I trust your judgment, Mimi. But be careful of Agoak. He may have turned into a brute, but he's still very, very intelligent. And he has an incredible sense of intuition."

"I'll be careful."

"We should get some of this meat back now, if only for appearances' sake."

They grabbed their axes and began taking swings at the frozen carcass. Judith felt so relieved at the idea of seeing an early end to her misery that she worked away with unusual vigor. Mimi went about her task with considerable care, but no less vigor than Judith. She looked forward to having some good bear meat to round out their diet. Both women were strong and they quickly piled up an impressive supply on the two sleds. When they had run out of space, and reached what they thought would be the limit of the dog's pulling power, they started back.

Before entering the igloo, Mimi searched around in a bundle which sat on her sled, found the bottle of pills and gave three to Judith.

"There," she said, "that's enough to make him sleep fifteen hours. All the time we need to get safely away from him."

They then slipped back into the igloo.

CHAPTER VI

Once the two women had gone, the igloo fell silent. The two children were fast asleep and Mimi had kept the baby in the hood of her anorak, so there was no noise but the crackling of the two wicks and the water simmering in the aluminum pan.

"People in Frobisher were very surprised," said Kigugtak all of a sudden.

"I suppose they must have been," Agoak said, bowing his head.

"There was a lot of talk about you among the Inuit. Every one I met had nothing but good things to say about you."

Agoak snickered.

"And then they all wondered how I could have done such a thing. And said how sorry they felt and what a pity it was. . . . Yes, I can hear them from here. Especially the Whites."

He went on to mock their English.

"Such a good Eskimo! How could he? You see why we shouldn't trust them."

Agoak shook his head.

"Yes, I'll bet they were full of fine words about how concerned and sympathetic they felt. . . . And they were feeling particularly sorry for Judith, I suppose?"

"Yes. And they still do."

"The thing is, I did it because of her."

"To be honest," said Kigugtak with a grave expression on his face, "I'd like to ask you the question."

"What's that?"

"Why did you do it?"

"Kill the two of them?"

"Not just that. You killed two men because they were raping your wife. I would've done the same thing. I don't think anybody would blame you for that. You might have got a short sentence, maybe a few months in prison. But as it was . . ."

"I tortured them," Agoak interrupted.

"Yes."

"Tell me honestly, Kigugtak, when you get into a temper, can you always keep it within reasonable limits?"

"I don't know . . . It seems to me . . . I wouldn't be . . ."

"I want you to be frank," Agoak interrupted again. "Have you never really seen red and flown right off the handle?"

"I guess so."

"If you walked in on two men who were in the middle of raping your wife and giving her a savage beating, wouldn't you do something about it?"

"Yes, I'd kill them."

"Is that all?"

"I don't know."

"Would you be seeing red? Would you be able to keep calm?"

"I honestly don't know."

"Well, I do. You just might do what I did. In fact, I think it's quite likely."

Kigugtak shook his head as he pondered the implications.

"But mutilating someone . . ."

"Yes, Kigugtak, you can mutilate and torture them because you just don't know what you're doing at that point! You lose your senses. And once you come to again, the horror's lying there staring you in the face. And you know there's nothing you can do to change it. Your ancestors were savages and regardless of what's happened to you in your life, you're a savage too, and always will be. And let me tell you something else. This isn't true just of us Inuit, or the Indians in the South. It's true of all men everywhere. There's no such thing as a civilized man. There are people who hear my story and are prepared to throw the first stone because they think they're pure. There are an awful lot of people like that. And if my story gets told twenty or thirty or one hundred years from now, there'll always be self-righteous people who'll act horrified. Well, do you ever watch television? Did you see the massacres that went on in Vietnam? Not conducted by Orientals, but by Americans, Whites, who think they're so perfect. What I did is nothing compared to what they get away with. . . . Even you are shocked by the things I did, Kigugtak. What I'm saying is that if you had been in that situation, you can't sit here and tell me you would have done nothing but shoot those two dead. You would've slashed and stabbed and hacked away at them until the blood came out in torrents. . . ."

Agoak paused for breath.

"Even with the bear a few days ago . . . I had to kill him. It was my life or his. But I couldn't blame him for what he tried to do to me. He was only trying to survive — and I happened to be a handy supply of meat! But it felt so good jabbing my knife into him over and over again!"

He pointed his finger at Kigugtak.

"And you would have felt the same!"

The two men fell silent again. Kigugtak sensed that Agoak was right. It's easy for someone who's not involved to make judgments from on high. But what happens when that someone finds himself confronted by the very same situation? Perhaps it was best not to draw any conclusions.

The two men sat staring into the flames fed by the two wicks. Then Kigugtak rummaged through the pocket of his anorak and pulled out a cigarette case.

"I hardly smoke anymore," he said, "but I still have a few cigarettes with me. Would you like one?"

Agoak held his open hand against the case.

"I smoked in Frobisher," he said, "but when I left I had to quit. If I start again, it'll make it more difficult later on. You understand, I'm sure."

"Yes, I do."

"I've still got a long road ahead of me, and I need all my strength."

"Are you tired of running?"

"It was bound to be unpleasant," replied Agoak with a nod. "Yes, I am tired. But there's nothing else I can do. I don't intend to go and rot in prison."

"They wouldn't hang you, they don't hang people anymore."

"I know. But they put them in prison for life, and that doesn't appeal to me either."

Agoak again looked at his guest in a rather strange way. As he spoke, his mouth twisted up and his voice took on a harsh tone.

"I'm going to keep on running," he said. "As long as I can. And I won't let anyone or anything get in my way or interfere with my plans."

He hit his thigh dramatically with his fist.

"Anything!" he repeated, nearly shouting.

Kigugtak was beginning to feel more and more uncomfortable. He realized he ought to steer the conversation in another direction, away from this very ticklish subject. In any case, they had now said pretty much all there was to say about it.

"Do you have weapons?" he asked Agoak. "Are you well equipped?"

"If the bear didn't ruin my rifle, and I don't think he did somehow, we've got two 12-gauge shotguns and two .303 rifles. I've also got some knives and a couple of good axes."

"What about ammunition?"

"I've got enough for the time being," Agoak replied with a sarcastic little laugh.

"I'm equipped about like you are," said Kigugtak, "except I've got three rifles, and almost two thousand cartridges, with what I just bought in Grise Fiord."

"You're a regular one-man army," said Agoak. "That's enough ammunition to last for quite a while."

"Yes, it is."

"I've also got some hides, quite a few in fact, and several spare anoraks. How about you?"

"Yes, I've got some hides. But the anoraks we're wearing are all we've got in the way of clothes."

"Do you want me to leave you a couple of others?" asked Kigugtak.

"No, that won't be necessary," said Agoak rather coolly. "But thanks for having thought of it." He then concluded, with a sweeping gesture of the arm, "Everything's going to work out, I'm sure of that now."

They heard some noise outside, the sound of muffled voices. The high-pitched one was clearly recognizable as Mimi's.

"That's the women coming back," said Kigugtak. "I hope they have some meat."

"They'd better, after all the time they've taken!" said Agoak.

The two women slipped back into the igloo, Judith first, followed immediately by Mimi, who went straight over to the children to see if they were still asleep.

"Look at them," she said, "they'll be waking up soon."

"I think we should have something to eat and then be off," said Kigugtak. "We've a long way to go, all the way to Baffin Island, almost to Pangnirtung."

"Did you get any bear meat?" asked Agoak.

"The two sleds are loaded with it," said Judith. "One for them and one for us."

She had brought in a piece of meat from the rump. She threw it into the boiling water and said, "We'll be able to enjoy this in a little while."

She approached Agoak.

"How's your fever?"

He shrugged his shoulders.

"It seems to be much better. It'll be better still once I've had something to eat."

"Are you hungry?"

"Yes."

Mimi had crouched down beside the bench, close to her children.

"It's a good sign when someone's hungry," she said.

She touched Agoak's forehead.

"He definitely feels less feverish. I've left some pills with Judith," she said, addressing Agoak. "I got them from the clinic in Frobisher. They're for fever and infection."

Kigugtak, who was sitting beside her, began to gesture with his hand, but Mimi turned around briskly and said in a measured tone of voice, "Isn't that so, Kigugtak?"

Agoak pulled a face, but Mimi didn't give him a chance to say anything.

"Sometimes the children need the odd bit of medication. So do I and my husband. You never know when you'll catch an infection and get a fever. That's what the pills are for. I left Judith three. That seems to be all you need to get back on your feet again."

Agoak drew the tip of his tongue across his lip as he looked at Mimi. He seemed unsure. He had a doubtful look in his eye.

"Agoak, you don't have to take them if you don't want to," said Judith. "But don't go complaining later on."

"I've never needed pills," said Agoak. "The Inuit have never needed pills. It was the Whites who made us sick."

"In this case, however, the Whites had nothing to do with it," Mimi observed with a laugh. "It was all the bear's fault. Mind you, he was white too! . . ."

Even Agoak had to laugh at Mimi's joke, and Judith was still chuckling as she prodded the meat in the pan.

"It's thawed out," she said. "Those who like it this way can eat. If you prefer it cooked, you'll have to wait a little longer."

Agoak plunged his hand in and took the first piece.

"I like it like this," he said.

"So do I," said Kigugtak as he helped himself. "Just barely thawed out and still cold on the inside, so you can enjoy it longer."

The women waited for theirs to cook, while the men chewed in silence. The children, who had suddenly woken up, wanted their share and were duly served.

Everyone ate his fill. When they were all finished, Judith made more tea, letting it boil a good while. Everyone enjoyed a cup, then Kigugtak got up and indicated it was time to leave.

"We have a lot of travelling still to do," he said. "Come."

They all went out the entrance, he first, then his family. Judith and Agoak followed behind. Kigugtak and Mimi made a final check of their baggage and, at the same time, of the dogs' leads. When everything was ready, the two kids sat down astride a couple of bundles and Kigugtak said his final farewell, which was echoed by Mimi and the children. The dogs strained against the heavily-laden sleds and once they started moving, the little convoy headed briskly towards the darkening eastern sky.

It was then that Judith first noticed the rifle in Agoak's hand.

"What's going on," she asked, "what are you doing with your gun?"

But Agoak was already aiming and taking his first shot. Judith lunged forward and tried to seize hold of him. Agoak responded by punching her right in the face and sending her sprawling on the ground, unconscious.

Agoak then set about systematically picking off each of the panic-stricken figures as they fled into the twilight. The massacre lasted only a few seconds and soon four bodies lay motionless on the snow. Agoak ran over to them to make sure they were all dead. When he got to Mimi, he saw something moving in her hood. He pulled it back to discover the baby and fired a bullet through its head. Meanwhile, the first lead dog had stopped amid the confusion and didn't know what to do next. Agoak pulled his lead up short and led both teams back to the igloo.

Judith, who was just coming to again, tried to get up. Her face was puffy and she had a large, bloody cut over one eyebrow.

"Agoak, why did you do that?! Why!" she screamed.

"Because they would have gone to Grise Fiord to get the police."

"That's not true! They'd just come back from Grise Fiord. They were going back to their own territory."

"How do you know? I'm telling you they'd have gone to Grise Fiord."

Feeling completely thunderstruck, Judith decided to say no more, unconvinced as she was by his assessment. Had all that education, all the training, succeeded only in making him a monster?

"Get into the igloo!" Agoak said, "Go on, get in!"

He pushed her in the direction of the igloo, then forced her to bend over and crawl in the entrance-way. He followed. Then, as he stood up again and went to sit down, Judith could see that the fever had returned. Feeling revolted but more clear-headed at the same time, she realized that losing her temper or showing any sign of remorse would serve no purpose, and might ruin the only chance she had left.

She collapsed not far from Agoak, who was propped up on one elbow with his head thrown back and having difficulty breathing. Judith decided the moment had perhaps come for her to play her last trump-card. It had to work, or she had no idea how she was going to extricate herself. Her only other choice was to submit to Agoak and go with him wherever he went, and the very prospect of that mortified her. Aware she might actually be risking death if she didn't make good her escape, Judith took the three pills from her pocket, poured out a burning cup of tea and moved close to Agoak.

"We have to leave tomorrow," she said. "We can't stay here any longer. If you get far enough away, nobody'll every suspect you killed Kigugtak and his family. But if we're going to leave, you have to get better. Take the pills."

Agoak looked surprised, then suspicious. But she was insistent and pressed the pills and the tea on him. Exhausted by the great stress he had just experienced and weakened by the infection which was on the rise instead of resolving, Agoak finally gave in. He swallowed the pills with a long gulp of hot tea, then wrapped himself up in the skins once again. He trembled all over as Judith stood beside him, keeping watch.

At one point Agoak turned his head in Judith's direction and asked in a thick voice, the words barely intelligible, "Did you do something to me?"

Judith touched his shoulder in what was meant to look like a gesture of tenderness.

"No, of course not," she said. "Go to sleep now."

Agoak buried his face in the furs.

Judith stayed close by him for some time after that, waiting for the pills to take effect. Agoak's breathing became slower and slower, and he had stopped moving about. Judith began to feel a great sense of relief and muttered a blessing for Mimi, who had never suspected, on giving Judith the medication, that she herself would so soon slip into a deep, untroubled sleep.

When she was finally convinced that her husband had been completely knocked out by the drug, Judith checked quickly around the igloo, took a little tea from the metal canister and left everything else in its place. Since Grise Fiord was close by, she needed only a bare minimum.

Outside, she unloaded everything from one of the sleds, even her gun. She needed to get away as fast as possible, because Agoak might always wake up: his brute strength and sheer force of will were not to be underestimated. As soon as there was the slightest let-up in the soporific effect of the pills, he might come to, make a supreme effort to shake off the last vestiges of sleep and manage to get his dog-team on Judith's trail. Her chances of outdistancing a pursuer were much better on an empty sled.

As an extra precaution, she undid three of Agoak's dogs and hitched them up with her team, leaving him only two. Out in the cold the whole process took longer than she thought it might, and a terrible sense of anguish began to gnaw away at her. It occurred to her to go back into the igloo and make sure that Agoak hadn't successfully conquered the effects of the drug. She knew only too well how intuitive the man was. She was almost certain that his sleep had already become fitful, and that something inside him was trying to rouse him from the torpor which held him down. But if she followed her instincts and went back to check on him, wouldn't she be taking an unnecessary risk?

Finally, the re-harnessing was nearly finished. She took hold of the last of the leather leads, which were extremely stiff with the cold, attached it to the remaining dog and stood up. She tiptoed over to the igloo and put her ear next to it. Suddenly the silence was broken by a kind of groaning.

Judith was alarmed. Agoak was surely fighting to wake up. She had to act quickly, push the dogs to the limits of their endurance and hope that if Agoak did wake up and managed to give chase, his two dogs wouldn't be capable of catching up with her team.

Judith ran back to the sled and brought the whip down hard on the dogs. She stood on the runners and looked back in the direction of the igloo, praying to all the saints and deities of her childhood, while her heart beat wildly. This was certainly her last chance. If ever fate was to smile on her, it had to be now. She was still glancing back at the igloo as she flailed away desperately at the dogs, who were pulling the near-empty sled along just about as fast as was possible.

Suddenly Judith let out a cry. Agoak had just crawled out of the igloo. He got up, looked around and seemed to spot her. Even from that far away Judith could see he was very unsteady on his legs. He staggered a couple of times, recovered his balance, then finally reached his sled, where he noticed the harnesses trailing on the ground from which Judith had removed the three dogs. Reduced to crawling on all fours, yet with a terrifying determination, Agoak tied up the extra leads, then moved towards the rear of the sled. Judith was steadily putting distance between them, but now that Agoak had overcome his cataleptic state, she felt considerably less confident about emerging victorious from this race against death. Worse still, he was now gulping down deep breaths of fresh air, which would soon dissipate the last of his drug-induced stupor. He seemed steadier on his legs already, and by the time he climbed onto the runners and began driving the dogs in Judith's direction, he seemed to be functioning more or less normally.

There was little doubt in Judith's mind that death would settle the race which was underway. The direction in which she was heading — straight for Grise Fiord — spoke eloquently of her intentions. It would mean the end for Agoak. He would never let her give herself up if he could help it. Judith was convinced he would kill her first.

She turned away and tightened her grip on the reins with one hand, while with the other she brought the whip down again and again. The dogs barked and occasionally howled with pain when struck by the whip, but they pulled the sled along as they had never pulled before.

Judith glanced back once or twice and noticed that despite Agoak's efforts, she was still a good distance from him. She saw to it her own dogs did not weaken for so much as a moment. She had the idea that as close as Grise Fiord seemed to be, the journey would take her at least twenty hours, if not more. Suddenly she realized the awful truth: the dogs would never last that long, they would have to stop. On the other hand, Agoak's dogs too would tire. Then what would happen? Would Agoak attempt to reach her on foot? If the time came, would she too have to flee on foot and try to lose herself in the Arctic twilight?

Suddenly a series of loud noises like explosions, off to the left, made Judith jump with fright. Two snowmobiles then appeared at the top of a snow dune, with all their lights on. Behind Judith, a shot rang out. Her heart beating wildly with hope now, Judith brought the dogs to a halt. One of the snowmobiles came towards her, while the other headed off in Agoak's direction. Judith could see that Agoak was taking aim with his rifle and she heard two more reports.

Just then, the snowmobile which had been headed her way pulled up. An officer of the RCMP stepped off the machine, dressed in the parka worn by all members of the force. He had his gun trained on her, but she raised her hands to show she was not armed and shouted at him in English, "Thank God you're here!"

The policeman was also an Eskimo, and spoke to her in Inuktitut, "Is that Agoak back there?"

"Yes."

"You must be Judith."

"Yes, that's right."

"Come with me."

He led her to his snowmobile and started off to where the others were. They could see Agoak taking aim on the other police officer. Suddenly there was another series of shots, fired in rapid succession. Agoak emptied his magazine and Judith watched horrified as the other policeman fell lifeless to the ground. The officer she was with yelled angrily, "Goddam it! Let's go!"

He gave his snowmobile full throttle, and they bumped along at top speed in Agoak's direction. Steering the vehicle as best he could with one hand, the policeman drew his revolver from his holster with the other, aimed and fired, but the bouncing motion of the snowmobile caused him to miss. He fired again, twice, three times, while Agoak, to whom they were getting closer and closer, methodically fired shot after shot. Suddenly Judith let loose a long shriek as the policeman she was with toppled off the speeding snowmobile. Before she could react and take control of the handlebars, the vehicle plowed into the igloo and destroyed it. She switched off the engine and sat paralyzed with fear and panic on the passenger seat.

Agoak lowered his gun and slowly came up to Judith. He said nothing, but gave her an implacable stare. With her throat choked up as if she were being strangled, she was incapable of speaking, while her extremities felt so lifeless she could only sit and endure Agoak's stare.

"Get up!" said Agoak.

There was no trace of sympathy in either his voice or his expression. He spoke to Judith as he might have spoken to an animal.

"Get up!" he said even more harshly.

In a slow, mechanical fashion, Judith began to stir. As she stood up, she was looking Agoak right in the eyes. He pointed to the two policemen.

"You see?" he said. "That's the end."

He backed away a short distance and found Judith's rifle where she had left it near the igloo. She had not counted on exchanging gunfire with Agoak during the course of her escape.

"This is your rifle, is it?" asked Agoak.

She nodded almost imperceptibly.

Agoak picked up the weapon, walked over to the policeman who had been riding in the snowmobile with Judith and kicked his foot. He stirred slightly, on the verge of death. Then Agoak took aim with his wife's weapon and fired point-blank into the policeman's body. He gave one last, terrible twitch before his muscles went slack. He was now quite dead.

"There," said Agoak with a cruel smile. "Do you know what I've just done?" he asked his wife.

She hunched up her shoulders, still too overcome with fear to say anything.

"They'll find the two bodies here. We'll be long gone, but they'll do a ballistics check on the bullets and that'll go into the record. If the day ever comes when they capture us, our guns'll be tested. They'll find out the two cops were killed with both our guns, mine and yours. You understand, Judith? You can tell them stories all you like, but you'll have no one to corroborate them. They just won't believe you. They'll take you for as much of a killer as me. And anybody who kills a policeman gets hanged. We'll both be hanged. Think about it, Judith. You and me. We're both in this mess together now. If you try to get away again, if you go to Grise Fiord or anywhere else to raise the alarm, you'll find the rope waiting for you."

He turned his back on Judith, climbed on one of the snowmobiles and drove off to where the bodies of Kigugtak and his family were lying. There he set about pillaging their belongings and finally came back with the dogs tied to the snowmobile, having left behind both the sleds and the supplies for which he had no use.

He returned to find Judith squatting on the ground. The dazed look on her face reflected the sense of profound bewilderment she felt inside. Gone was any further thought of revolt, any willingness to risk escape. Suddenly, everything had collapsed around her. She was alone once again with Agoak, trapped in a situation which, this time, was utterly without hope. The man was simply too clever to be outwitted. He knew how to exploit the slightest advantage. And he had finally found a way to make his wife buckle under, so that she would never be a threat to him again.

Judith felt crushed by the very thought of what lay ahead of her.

There was no longer any way out, and there might never be again. There was always the chance they might be captured, but if they were, no matter what she did, no matter what she said, the final outcome would be the same. Outwitting the other police officers who would now be deploying major resources in an effort to capture them, would mean living the primitive life under the orders of a man who had become a stranger to all morality, pity and human sentiment. What, she asked herself again, what had become of the loving, considerate, hard-working husband, the model Eskimo, that Judith had once known in a distant past, which now seemed to her utterly unreal?

Agoak stood with his hands on his hips gazing at their camp, the wrecked igloo, the snowmobiles, the bodies.

"They travel in pairs," he said thoughtfully. "It'll take some time before another pair is sent out and they find these two."

He turned to Judith.

"Get the snowmobile out of there," he said, "and rebuild the igloo. We're going to stay here for two or three days, then move on."

There was a further possibility which Agoak didn't much like, namely that this team of policemen might be supported by another. They had perhaps felt close to a capture and asked for some back-up. Still another, and equally unpleasant, possibility was that the dead policemen had spotted Agoak's camp from some distance and radioed in its location, so that the police could now find Agoak quickly once they decided to make their move. Agoak therefore decided to put a bold plan into operation.

First of all he bullied Judith into hurrying along with her work, then went to examine the snowmobile which had attempted the first assault and was sitting nearby. On it he found a long-distance radio-telephone. He searched through the dead constable's clothing and pulled out his ID. His name was Theo Akunak, an Inuk, one of a certain number employed by the RCMP in the Arctic. Agoak studied the communication device. Though no expert in such matters, he had no trouble finding the switch to activate the radio. His rudimentary knowledge also told him that the wavelength of the transmitter was probably set for a particular receiver. He hesitated only momentarily before picking up the microphone, switching the set on and pressing the red button marked CALL. A voice replied almost immediately, through a steady background of static. Agoak, trying to make himself heard over the noise, shouted, "Akunak speaking: Hello, Akunak, over."

"This is base control. Go ahead Akunak."

The conversation was brief. Fortunately, all the static interference made it difficult to recognize voices. Agoak learned that in fact Akunak had been in communication with base control earlier to report that he had sighted Agoak's camp. Agoak himself now denied this, however, explaining that he had simply mistaken another Eskimo for the wanted man.

Base control, on the other hand, told him exactly what he didn't wish to hear: another squad of four policemen, travelling on two snowmobiles, was leaving that same day to come to the assistance of the district patrol, since there were no extra men available in Grise Fiord.

When the communication ended, Agoak did some calculating. If the policemen were coming from Frobisher, it would take them at least four days travelling at forty kilometres an hour, or even slightly faster, before they got too close. Agoak could get away with staying another two days, which would give him enough time to bring his debilitating fever under control. At that point he would be on his way again, and counting on the dogs to do their utmost.

This time, however, Agoak planned to strike out in a different direction. He would head back towards Baffin Island, taking a wide sweep around the mouth of the fiord, and then head inland for the mountains. Once winter had returned, he would use the cover of successive blizzards to get to the mountains on Ellesmere Island.

Agoak noticed that Judith seemed to be making little progress with the blocks for the igloo. He walked up behind her and, without warning, gave her a violent kick, which caused her to go flying face first into the snow.

"I want that igloo up today, not tomorrow!" he yelled at her. "Stop dawdling and get to work."

Judith had the urge to fling back some reply, but, realizing it would get her nowhere, she simply lowered her head and went back to work. Agoak watched her for a little while, then began checking through their supplies and stacking them on the sleds, adding to what they already had the belongings he had looted from Kigugtak. He was particularly pleased with the boxes of cartridges. There was a supply to last a long time. The traps would also come in very handy. He smiled at the thought of the good summer living he could look forward to in the mountains of Baffin Island. It was a little too close to civilization, but there were sure to be caves or rock ledges which would conceal them from any spotter planes. And as the cold weather set in again they would move still farther north, Judith and he each with their own sled to look after. Not only did he now have Kigugtak's dogs as replacements for any of his that might die, but he had also helped himself to his victim's weapons, as well as a whole stack of large, warm furs and several extra anoraks. Agoak might even have some problem figuring out how to fit all these supplies onto just two sleds. It had occurred to him to try travelling with three sleds, but try as he might, he just couldn't see how it would be possible, especially if they found they had to travel at speed. There were, of course, the snowmobiles, but that would mean leaving both the sleds and the dogs behind, and besides, the fuel that was in the two vehicles would not take them very far. Agoak quickly gave up on that idea.

By the time Agoak had finished sorting and packing all the supplies, Judith had finished the igloo. While rebuilding it she had come across the stone lamp, tripod and pan which they used for heating water. Without consulting Agoak, Judith went into the igloo, got three wicks going in the lamp, went outside again to get some snow and put it in the pan to melt.

Agoak came in behind her, carrying two rifles and two boxes of ammunition. He sat down on the ground, checked the magazines and filled them both with cartridges. Judith went outside to rummage through all the baggage and finally came upon the caribou meat which had belonged to Mimi. It would be gloomier than ever inside the igloo, what with the usual extended silences and the now irrevocable estrangement between the two of them, but at least the food would be more agreeable. As she enjoyed the caribou Judith would be thinking of Kigugtak and his family, who had been shot down in cold blood by a homicidal maniac, a madman who, until quite recently, had been one of the shining hopes of his race. . . .

But there was no use regretting that anymore. Judith simply had nothing to look forward to, nothing but a bottomless pit of misery. A sudden twinge of pain in her abdomen reminded her of the baby she was carrying and this in itself was a source of great sadness to her. What was the point of bringing this child into the world? What sort of life lay ahead of him fleeing from the police in the company of a brutish father, a confirmed killer without a conscience who was completely insensitive to the most basic feelings of those around him?

Another, more noticeable twinge threw Judith into a panic. A sharp pain shot through her, followed by a sudden sense of release in her lower abdomen. Her pants were soaked through. She got up quickly, went outside to get a clean hide, came back in immediately, stretched the hide out on the bench and took off her boots and pants.

Then she put on the felt boots she had brought back into the igloo along with the fur. Agoak looked up to see what she was doing.

"What's going on?" he asked.

"It's the baby," replied Judith. "He's ready." She wiped herself with a rag she had in her pocket. Agoak looked a little more interested than usual. He sat up.

"Make some tea," said Judith.

She surprised even herself with the peremptory tone in which she had given the order. She was no less surprised, indeed she was astonished, to see Agoak get up, place the pot on its stand and put the tea and boiling water in it. He knelt down and kept an eye on the beverage as it brewed. When the first curls of the brown liquor began to appear and the water reached the boil again, Agoak poured out a cup and handed it to Judith.

The hide she had brought in to lie on had been frozen, but she stretched it right out and, despite being naked from the waist down, managed to hollow out a little nest for her buttocks. She took a long gulp of her tea and lay down again with her eyes closed. She was seized by another pain. She tightened up, felt the pain ease and let out a long sigh. She knew the birth would not take very long. She could tell from the frequency of the contractions that the child would soon be out. She had done so much walking, snowshoeing and hard physical labor in the preceding eight months that she had developed all the muscles she needed for a quick, effortless birth.

The next contraction prompted a hoarse groan from her. Agoak stood watching her nearby.

"Is there anything I should do?" he asked.

Judith was taken aback by the question. After treating her no better than an animal for all this time, he was now being nothing less than considerate.

But Judith did not get carried away. She knew only too well what cruel changes of heart Agoak was capable of. She would not let this momentary show of interest mislead her into trusting his feelings again.

"When the time comes," she said, "you can cut the cord. If you don't want to, I'll do it."

This time the pain made her cry out, her stomach contracted, she cried out again and the baby was there, launched forward by another powerful contraction of her well-exercised muscles. She had given birth pretty much in the typical Eskimo fashion, except that having come a little late to this life of hard work, she had experienced enough pain to make her cry out once or twice. The child, in any case, had come, and Agoak, to Judith's further surprise, was busy tying and cutting the cord. Then, there was silence.

The brand-new, helpless creature who had just emerged from Judith's stomach in this icy igloo, was a girl.

Long ago, Agaguk's father, Agoak's great-grandfather, had killed an Inuk from Pangnirtung for having stolen some of his pelts, and had been forced to flee the police, taking with him the Montagnais woman he had made his wife. A girl had been born to him, like this one, and he had killed it. Later Agaguk was born and he had been spared. Now, decades later, Agoak, who had once been an educated man with a brilliant future, found himself in a similar situation. He too was fleeing from the police and eking out a bare existence on his long journey. A girl had been born to him and all she represented was a useless, extra mouth to feed, a burden, an imposition. Agoak could not defy destiny a moment longer; he knew in his guts what he had to do. He took the bloody mass of flesh which lay between Judith's thighs and dashed out its brains on the butt of his gun. Judith let out a long, hoarse scream, a sound full of visceral terror.

Agoak stood beside her with his hands on his hips and said calmly "Get up and make us something to eat. The police are on our tail, we have to get out of here as soon as possible."

Judith pulled herself to her feet and, with an ax, began chopping up pieces of caribou meat on the icy ground. Nearby, Agoak was crouched down cleaning his rifle with an oily rag.

The wheel had come full circle.